"Why do you want me

"You're the best assis

"You want me back so I can be your shadow, following you around, be at your beck and call. Well, I'm not your pet, Ayden."

"I never thought you were." And he sounded offended that she thought so. "And I've never treated you like one. You've always been a valuable employee."

Maya shook her head. So he was just going to act like it never happened? That they'd never seen each other naked? That they hadn't slept together on the thick white rug in front of his fireplace?

"You should go, Ayden." She pushed at his rock-hard chest, which was darn near impenetrable, and walked to the door.

"Why?" He grasped both her hands in his. His eyes were fire when he said, "You haven't even heard me out."

"Why should I, Ayden? I left for a reason and you damn well know why."

* * *

St

Dear Reader,

At the CEO's Pleasure is the first book in a compelling new series titled The Stewart Heirs. The idea for the trilogy came from watching episodes of the '80s soap opera *Dynasty* and the current presidential drama. I wondered what it must be like for Trump's oldest children when he started a new family and had other children.

Our hero, Ayden Stewart, is the eldest son, the black sheep, whose father, Henry Stewart, abandoned him and his mother to start a new family. Ayden has become successful in his own right, but is looking for his father's approval, which he never gains. Instead, he's drawn to his capable assistant, Maya Richardson, who shares his feelings of being an outcast in her own family after her sister slept with her boyfriend. I hope you root for these two lost souls coming together to not only find an off-the-charts chemistry, but a love for the ages.

Want to know when Fallon Stewart's story will be released or learn about my other books? Visit my website and sign up for my newsletter at yahrahstjohn.com, or write me at yahrah@yahrahstjohn.com.

Enjoy,

Yahrah St. John

YAHRAH ST. JOHN

AT THE CEO'S PLEASURE

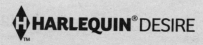

Recycling programs
for this product may
not exist in your area.

ISBN-13: 978-1-335-60342-5

At the CEO's Pleasure

Copyright © 2018 by Yahrah Yisrael

Printed in U.S.A.

Yahrah St. John is the author of twenty-nine books. When she's not at home crafting one of her spicy romances featuring compelling heroes and feisty heroines with a dash of family drama, she is gourmet cooking or traveling the globe seeking out her next adventure. St. John is a member of Romance Writers of America. Visit www.yahrahstjohn.com for more info.

Books by Yahrah St. John

Harlequin Desire

The Stewart Heirs
At the CEO's Pleasure

Harlequin Kimani Romance

Cappuccino Kisses
Taming Her Tycoon
Miami After Hours
Taming Her Billionaire
His San Diego Sweetheart

Visit her Author Profile page at
Harlequin.com for more titles.

To my agent, Christine Witthohn, for her hard work
in helping me move to the Desire line.

One

Ayden Stewart stared out at the Austin city skyline from the fiftieth floor of Stewart Investments. It had taken him fifteen years since graduating from Harvard to build his company, but at thirty-six, he'd finally achieved his goal. And he'd done it all on his own. Without the help of his father, Henry Stewart, a rich man who'd never bothered to acknowledge his eldest son's existence, not after his second wife had given him two heirs for his own company, Stewart Technologies. It was just as well. He'd long ago stopped looking for love and acceptance from his old man.

Knock. Knock. Knock.

"Come in." His office door opened and his assistant, Carolyn Foster, walked in. The statuesque blonde wore pregnancy well; barely a baby bump could be seen in the smart attire she wore.

"Do you have a minute?"

"Of course," Ayden responded, moving away from the window. "What can I do for you?"

"I have some not so pleasant news to deliver," Carolyn said.

"Oh, yeah? Whatever it is, just give it to me straight, no chaser."

"Very well…" She paused for several beats. "I won't be coming back after my maternity leave in a few months."

"Excuse me?" This couldn't be happening to him *again*.

"I'm sorry, Ayden—really, I am—but my husband and I have been trying for some time to start a family. And, well, I just want to enjoy the time with our first child because I'm not sure when we might have another."

Carolyn would make a fantastic mother because she was already putting her child first. It made Ayden think of the only person who'd ever cared one iota about him, who was gone, taken away too soon. His mother Lillian Stewart-Johnson, God rest her soul, had passed away several years ago from a heart attack. He suspected his mother's illness had been caused by years of stress and abuse at the hands of his stepfather Jack Johnson. Jack was a habitual smoker and a mean drunk.

Ayden had focused hard on his studies, so he could get the hell out of the house. And he'd been lucky. In junior high, his teachers recognized his high IQ and had helped Ayden receive a scholarship to a prestigious boarding school in the East. From there, his grades helped him get into Harvard and he'd never looked back.

Growing up, Ayden had developed a thick skin. He'd had to in order to live in the Johnson household, and not just because of the bruises, but because of the lack of love or affection. He'd learned he didn't need either. If he hadn't met his roommate, Luke Williams, in boarding school in the ninth grade, who knows how long Ayden would have gone without any real feelings. Ayden's goal had been to save his mama from working two jobs to support Jack's pack-and-bottle-a-day habit, but it had been useless. By the time he'd finally started making enough money, his mother was gone and he was all alone in the world except for Luke, his closest friend. Why had his mother let men bully her all her life? First, Henry had intimidated her into a small settlement, cutting her out of her rightful shares in Stewart Technologies. Then, Jack spent the little money she had received. Why hadn't she fought for the child support she was entitled to?

"I imagine there's nothing I could do to change your mind?" Ayden inquired. He knew it was a long shot, but he couldn't understand why anyone would throw away a good-paying job in order to stay home and change poopy diapers. Carolyn's departure was going to leave him in quite a pickle. One he hadn't been in since a certain uptight but beautiful assistant had left him five years ago.

"No, there isn't," Carolyn said, "but we can find a replacement. You always said you never thought you'd find someone as good as Maya and look what happened—you hired me."

He would never forget the day, ten years ago, when Maya Richardson had walked through his door looking for a job. She'd been a godsend, helping Ayden grow Stewart Investments into the company it was today. Thinking of her brought a smile to Ayden's face. How could it not? Not only was she the best assistant he'd ever had, Maya had fascinated him. Utterly and completely. Maya had hidden an exceptional figure beneath professional clothing and kept her hair in a tight bun. But Ayden had often wondered what it would be like to throw her over his desk and muss her up. Five years ago, he hadn't gone quite that far, but he had crossed a boundary.

Maya had been devastated over her breakup with her boyfriend. She'd come to him for comfort, and, instead, Ayden had made love to her. Years of wondering what it would be like to be with Maya had erupted into a passionate encounter. Their one night together had been so explosive the next morning Ayden had needed to take a step back to regain his perspective. He'd had to put up his guard; otherwise, he would have hurt her badly. He thought he'd been doing the right thing, but Maya hadn't thought so. In retrospect, Ayden wished he'd never given in to temptation. But he had, and he'd lost a damn good assistant. Maya had quit, and Ayden hadn't seen or heard from her since.

Shaking his head, Ayden strode to his desk and

picked up the phone, dialing the recruiter who'd helped him find Carolyn. He wasn't looking forward to this process. It had taken a long time to find and train Carolyn. Before her, Ayden had dealt with several candidates walking into his office thinking they could ensnare him.

No, he had someone else in mind. A hardworking, dedicated professional who could read his mind without him saying a word and who knew how to handle a situation in his absence. Someone who knew about the big client he'd always wanted to capture but never could attain. She also had a penchant for numbers and research like no one he'd ever seen, not even Carolyn.

Ayden knew exactly who he wanted. He just needed to find out where she'd escaped to.

"Aren't you tired yet?" Callie Lewis asked Maya Richardson after they'd jogged nearly five miles in the muggy San Antonio weather. They'd met up at 6:00 a.m. after Maya had stumbled out of bed, placed her shoulder-length black hair in a ponytail, and put on her favorite sports tank with built-in bra and running shorts.

"No. Not yet." Maya hazarded a glance at Callie. Her friend was five foot two and nearly two hundred pounds, and had been following an intense exercise routine to lose weight. She'd already lost fifty pounds and Maya was trying to encourage her. They'd been best friends ever since Callie had defended Maya from bullies in the fifth grade, so Callie's well-being was important to her.

"Well, I need to stop a sec," Callie paused midstride. She limped over to a nearby bench and began a series of stretches.

"Okay, no problem." Maya jogged in place while she stretched.

"What's got you all riled up?" Callie asked. "You've been on edge for a couple of days."

Maya stopped jogging and stood still. She'd been trying to outrun the past, which was impossible, but she was giving it the old college try. "I received an invitation from Raven and Thomas for Nysha's baptism."

"You received what?" Callie's brown eyes grew large with amazement.

"You heard me."

"I just can't believe your sister and that sleazy husband of hers had the nerve to send it. Not after what they did to you."

Maya shrugged. It had been five long years since she'd felt the sting of Raven's betrayal with her boyfriend, Thomas. If anyone had told her that her baby sister would steal her man and marry him, she would have called them a liar. Maya and Raven had always been so close. When their father had left their mother, it had broken up their family, leaving her mom Sophia alone to support them. It hadn't been easy especially because her mother favored Raven.

"How can you be silent about this?"

"Because... I've made my peace, Callie," Maya replied. "I had to. They got *married*, for Christ's sake. I didn't have much choice."

"You didn't go to their wedding."

"How could I? Back then it was all too fresh."

"Including what happened between you and Ayden?"

Maya rolled her eyes. "Let's not talk about him, okay?"

"Why not? If I recall what you said back then, it was the best sex you'd ever had in your life," Callie said, making air quotes. "Yet after your night with him and his failure to acknowledge what happened, you quit your dream job."

Maya sighed heavily. She wished she'd kept that secret to herself. Five years ago, for better or for worse, her life had changed. She'd accepted it and moved on.

She began running in place again. "C'mon, my muscles are starting to tense up. We have to finish our run."

"You go on ahead," Callie stated. "I'm going to sit this one out. I'll call you later."

"Sure thing." Maya jogged off in the opposite direction. As she did, she thought back to that horrible night.

She'd been working late because Ayden needed a presentation for the following day. She'd picked up takeout to bring to her boyfriend, Thomas. Using the key he'd given her, she'd opened the door to his town house and found it dark. It was surprising, given his car was sitting in the driveway. After placing the bags on the kitchen counter, she'd heard voices.

Who was visiting Thomas? It was well after eight o'clock, so Maya had walked upstairs to investigate. She'd never forget the sight that greeted her: her baby sister, Raven, on top of Thomas as they writhed on the bed. Maya had screamed bloody murder. Raven had rushed off the bed to the bathroom while Thomas tried to cover himself with a sheet as he'd attempted to explain. What was there to discuss? She'd caught him banging her sister. Maya had rushed out of the room, damn near falling down the stairs and losing a great shoe in the process to make it to her car. Fumbling with the key, she'd eventually started it up and was pulling off when Raven came running out the door in Thomas's shirt calling after her. The whole incident had been humiliating.

How long had their affair been going on?

How long had both of them been laughing behind her back?

Maya ran harder. Faster. But she couldn't outrun the memories. They must have really thought she was a fool for believing his lies that she was the kind of girl he wanted to marry. Her mother was right. Raven was the beauty in the family.

That was the state she'd been in when she'd arrived on Ayden's doorstep. Maya hadn't known where else to go. Callie lived in San Antonio and Maya had just lost her sister to a man she thought she loved. Over the five years of their working relationship, she and Ayden had shared some personal stories, especially when he'd told her about his past; she'd hoped he could lend her an ear now when she needed someone to listen.

Ah, Ayden. He'd been her secret crush for years before she'd met Thomas. When she'd started working for him, Maya had thought the sun and moon hung on the green-eyed devil, but Ayden hadn't seen her like that, like a woman. All he saw was a smart, efficient PA who did his bidding—which included making reservations for his dates with beautiful women, and sending them expensive flowers or trinkets as a parting gift when he was done with them. And yet, she'd chosen to go to Ayden, the man who didn't believe in love and thought it was a hoax meant to sell greeting cards.

That night, he'd offered her comfort. A shoulder to cry on. Comfort in ways she'd never been able to forget. Initially, he'd been shocked by her disheveled presence on his doorstep, but as soon as he'd seen her puffy, red-rimmed eyes, Ayden had immediately taken her into his embrace and closed the door behind him. He'd sat her down on the couch and listened as she'd told him of Raven and Tom's betrayal, of her failure. No one was ever going to love her, *want* her. She was a nothing. A nobody. A plain Jane that no man would ever be compelled to marry. Ayden had refused to hear of it. Had told her she was wrong. He'd stroked her hair and told her everything was going to be all right. With tears in her eyes, she'd glanced up at him, and then she'd done something desperate. She'd kissed him.

The surprising thing was he hadn't pushed her away. Instead, he'd kissed her back. One thing had led to another and the next moment, she and Ayden were making love on his bear skin rug on the floor of his living room. To this day, Maya had never been able to fully understand what had happened. One minute, he'd been consoling her and telling her she was beautiful and worthy of love, and the next, she'd been wrapped in his arms having wild, passionate sex.

It had literally been the most exciting sexual encounter of her life. Maya had experienced true bliss and one hell of an orgasm, but as soon as it was over, Ayden had pulled away. What she'd thought was heaven on earth had soon turned into a nightmare. Ayden told her he hadn't meant for it to happen. Maya had been crushed for the second time in one night. She'd dressed as fast as she could and had left to lick her wounds in private.

She'd relived that moment many nights since, wondering how their relationship had taken such a turn. Maya had always harbored feelings for Ayden in the past, but she'd never thought for a second that they were reciprocated. She'd eventually come to the conclusion that he'd made love to her out of pity because she'd been so pathetic. Knowing how he felt, Maya couldn't face Ayden again and had tendered her resignation.

Looking back, Maya realized that she'd been more upset over Ayden's rejection than Thomas's. Sure, she'd been hurt by Thomas because she'd loved him, but it had been her sister stealing her man that hurt the most. She'd never forgiven Raven, and they hadn't spoken in five years. It was Ayden who'd really broken her heart.

Once Maya had pushed herself to the limit with ten miles, she stopped running. It was time she faced the past with her sister so she could move forward with her life. And there was no better time than the present.

* * *

"Do you think she'll come back?" Ayden asked his best friend on a transatlantic call later that evening. It was before 7:00 a.m. in London, but he knew Luke Williams would already be up. How did he know? Because they were alike—notorious workaholics and driven to succeed. Luke was a financial analyst making millions.

"After the way you treated her when she left?" Luke said. "I wouldn't."

Ayden frowned. "Was I really that bad?"

"Hmm, I don't know, let me think," Luke paused for dramatic effect. "You were a slave driver at the office, rarely giving the poor girl a day off. And at a moment of weakness, you shag her and then tell her to kick rocks. I dunno, I might have a problem with that."

"Thanks a lot, Luke."

"You did call me, you know," Luke responded. "If you didn't want me to keep it one hundred with you then you should have called another mate."

"You're my only *mate*." Ayden replied. He didn't have many friends. He'd never had the time to make any because he was too busy pushing himself to excel, to make something of himself despite Henry Stewart turning his back and leaving him and his mom with an abusive stepfather.

"Yeah, that's true. No one else can tolerate you. Except maybe Maya, and you made a royal mess of that relationship."

"I know I messed up, but I can fix it."

Luke snorted. "By offering Maya her job back?

Why on earth would she ever agree? What does she get out of it?"

"I'm prepared to offer her a generous salary."

"And if she wants more?"

"What do you mean?"

"C'mon, man, don't be an idiot. Maya left because you two slept together. If you offer her a job, she might be thinking there's more on the table."

Ayden had never thought Maya might want more. "I'm not prepared to give her anything else. You know how I feel about love, marriage, the whole white-picket-fence thing."

"Yeah, yeah, sing to the choir. I've already heard this bit before," Luke stated. "Poor you, your dad left your mom to marry a hot tart, leaving you and your mom with nothing."

"That's right. Love is for other poor dumb schmucks."

"Like me, you mean," Luke countered.

Darn. He'd stuck his foot in his mouth. Luke had just married a beautiful redhead named Helena and they were head over heels in love. But if anyone could make a go of marriage, it was Luke. "Present company excluded," Ayden stated.

Luke chuckled. "You've never minced words before, Ayden, so don't start now."

"Helena is lovely," Ayden replied. "And she's madly in love with you. She can't wait to have a mess of babies with you."

"That's right, my friend. I'll have Helena knocked up before the year is out," Luke said, laughing. "That way she can't leave me for another man when she realizes she married a dumb schmuck like me."

Ayden laughed. That's what he loved about Luke. He could be self-deprecating and still be the life of the party. "So let's return to my original point for this call."

"What was that again?"

"Maya. And what it would take for her to agree to come back to me, I mean, the position of executive assistant at Stewart Investments."

"You would have to find the right incentive that doesn't include becoming a notch on your bedpost."

"That's not going to happen again," Ayden said. "Bedding Maya was a one-time thing. Plus, I doubt she's been carrying a torch for me. For Christ's sake, it was only one night!"

"If you say so, my friend. I've given my advice, for what it's worth. Good luck, and let me know how it turns out."

"Will do." Ayden ended the call and stared down at the folder in his lap. It held the address of where Maya was staying in Austin. He'd hired a private investigator to research her whereabouts. His timing was perfect because she was back in town for her niece's baptism and staying at a downtown hotel.

Ayden had to admit he was shocked by what he'd read in the file. He recalled how devastated Maya had been the night she'd come to him after discovering her sister in bed with her boyfriend. If she was returning, it had to mean she'd forgiven them. Surely that meant good news for him? He could ask her to come back to

Stewart Investments, and things would be different between them now. After all, it had been years since Ayden had seen her. Although he might have had the odd fantasy about her, on his part, any residual feelings from their night together five years ago were long gone. Ayden had been with many women since Maya. More beautiful. More stunning.

He and Maya had always enjoyed an excellent working relationship. He was certain they could get past this if she was willing to forgive him for his lack of sensitivity and give them another chance. He knew it was a long shot, but there was only one way to find out. He had to go to her, and he wasn't leaving until her answer was yes.

From the bathroom of the Baptist church, Maya fretted as she smoothed down the dress she'd chosen to wear to Nysha's baptism. Should she have come?

Throughout the years, Raven had tried to extend an olive branch, but Maya had rebuffed each and every effort. Why? Because Maya was jealous. Raven was living the life that should have been hers. If she was honest, Maya would have loved that life with Ayden, but he hadn't wanted her five years ago. Or not in the way she'd hoped.

So why come back?

Because she couldn't go on living this way, holding on to past hurts and hiding away from the world. It was time to move on with her life. She'd come to make peace with her sister.

She glanced at herself in the mirror. The sleeveless

plum dress had a deep V showing a swell of cleavage, thanks to the push-up bra she'd spent a fortune on in the hopes it would give her a bosom. Her long black hair, her best feature, was coiffed and hung in big curls down her back. She'd even allowed her hair stylist, who doubled as a makeup artist, to do her face. After all these years, she had to look her best because, Lord knows, her mother would be in full diva mode. Raven, of course, wouldn't have to try hard because she was naturally beautiful.

And now it was time to face the music. She couldn't very well hang out in the church bathroom forever. Grabbing her clutch purse, she made for the door. Sophia Richardson was greeting guests at the church entrance. From where Maya stood, she noted her mother's stylish salt-and-pepper updo and what looked like her Sunday-best suit, complete with pumps. But rather than looking the picture of a radiant grandma, her mother had lost weight and appeared a bit gaunt with sunken cheeks. Her normal caramel skin looked sallow.

Maya braced herself as she walked toward her. "Mother."

"Maya?" On cue, Sophia looked her over from head to toe—from the designer sandals to the simple Marc Jacobs sheath to the designer handbag. Apparently she passed muster, because her mother said, "I'm happy you've finally chosen to put the past behind you and return to the fold."

She held open her arms and Maya reluctantly walked into them. As expected, the embrace was brief. Maya suspected she'd received it because several guests had walked in and her mother wouldn't dare make a scene.

"Raven and Thomas will be so happy to see you," Sophia whispered in her ear. "Please go in." She motioned Maya toward the pews.

Would they be happy to see her? Or would her presence be a reminder of their past transgressions? Maya forced herself to put one foot in front of the other and enter the hall. Raven and Thomas were at the end of the aisle talking with the pastor. Her sister looked as stunning as ever even though she'd just had the baby two months ago. She was wearing a cream suit and had her hair in a French roll. Raven was already back to her svelte size-six figure. Thomas wore a suit and striped tie and beamed by her side, holding the baby.

Maya walked toward them. When Raven turned around and saw Maya, Maya felt her heart constrict. It had hurt being estranged from her baby sister.

"Maya?" Raven said as she drew near.

Maya glanced at Thomas and gave him a nod, stepping toward Raven. "Yes, I'm here."

Tears welled in her sister's eyes. "Oh, thank God, our prayers were answered. I've asked God for forgiveness every day for what we—" she glanced at her husband "—did to you. And now, I'm blessed to have you back in my life, in our daughter's life."

"Don't get carried away, Raven," Maya responded. "All is not swept under the rug."

"Of course not," Raven said. "I owe you a long overdue apology." She reached for Maya's hands and grasped them in her own. "I'm so sorry for hurting you, Maya. Can you please find it in your heart to forgive me?"

Maya stared at her in stunned disbelief. She had never expected an apology. Least of all, from Raven, who'd always been self-centered. But then again she'd never given her the chance.

"We're both sorry," Thomas said from Raven's side. "You deserved better than how we treated you. You deserved the truth. We should never have sneaked behind your back. It was wrong and I'm sorry."

Maya swallowed and nodded. She was too overcome to speak. She didn't know what she'd thought would happen during the visit, but clearly Raven and Thomas had matured enough to admit their mistakes.

"Would you like to meet your niece?" Raven asked, tears brimming in her eyes.

"Y-yes, I'd like that very much."

Raven walked over to Thomas, took their daughter out of his arms and placed the sleeping baby in Maya's. Her niece was the most beautiful little girl Maya had ever seen, with her smooth brown skin and shock of hair surrounded by a white headband with a bow. She was outfitted in the cutest white lace baptism dress. "She's beautiful." Maya grasped her niece's little finger in her hand.

"Can you believe I'm a mom?" Raven asked in wonder.

"Actually, I can't," Maya said, glancing her way, "but you are."

Raven gave a halfhearted smile. "You were always supposed to be the stay-at-home wife while I was supposed to be the career girl. It's funny how the tide changes."

"Yes, it's funny." Maya leaned over and returned Nysha into her sister's arms. "She's really beautiful. Congratulations to you both."

Maya stepped away as fast as humanly possible. It didn't hurt that guests were already headed toward them to greet the happy family. She needed some air. She couldn't breathe; it felt like she was suffocating. Maya sidestepped several guests entering the church and rushed outside.

Leaning against the building, she took in large gulps of air and forced the rising tide of emotions overwhelming her to calm. Had she honestly thought it would be easy seeing Raven and Thomas with their daughter? Maya glanced at the door. It should have been her. She should be the one who was a wife and mother; it's what she'd always wanted. Maya had always known she would make a good mom because she'd cared for Raven her entire life. Sophia Richardson had been too busy working two or, sometimes, three jobs to be there for them. Maya had been left to care for Raven, make her dinner, help with her homework and pick out her school clothes. So much so that Raven once had called her Mommy. Sophia had been livid and had yelled at Raven that *she* was her mommy.

Maternal instinct ran through Maya's veins, while Raven had never cared for another human being beside herself until now. But it was clear to Maya that

Raven loved her daughter and was happy. Maya didn't begrudge her sister happiness, but did it have to come at her expense? Perhaps she'd made a mistake in attending? She could sneak off with no one being the wiser. She'd made an appearance. Surely that had to count for something?

Maya was just about to head down the church steps when her mother's voice rang out. "Maya, dear, we're about to begin."

Darn. She'd missed her chance to use her get-out-of-jail-free card.

Inhaling, Maya spun around to face her mother and walked inside the church.

Hours later, Maya was looking for her handbag in one of the many bedrooms of Nysha's godparents' home. She was ready to leave. After the baptism ceremony, the entire group had adjourned here for a light meal. True to form, Sophia had gushed over their home, how beautiful it was and what great godparents they would make. It made Maya ill to see that nothing had changed; her mother was just as superficial as she'd been before.

Maya had done her part by showing up and making polite pleasantries. It was time for her to leave.

"Ah, there it is," she said aloud when she discovered her purse.

"Do you have a minute?" a male voice said from behind her.

Maya didn't need to turn around to know who it belonged to. They'd once been lovers. She whirled on her heel to face Thomas. If looks could kill, he would have been struck down on the spot. "What do you want?"

Thomas held up his hands in a defensive posture. "I'm sorry. I didn't mean to scare you."

"You didn't."

"I was hoping I could speak to you for a few minutes."

"I don't wish to discuss the past," Maya responded. Just being with her family had conjured enough of her old insecurities.

Thomas lowered his eyes. "Quite frankly, neither do I. It wasn't my finest moment."

"Then what is it that you want? I don't have all day."

Thomas glanced up and Maya hated to see the regret in his eyes. But she wasn't prepared for his next words. "It's about Sophia."

Maya's ears perked up. "What about my mother?"

"You may have noticed she's lost some weight?"

"Yes, I did, but I figured maybe she was dieting for the big event," Maya offered. It wasn't completely out of the realm of possibility. Her mother believed in looking her best, especially when the spotlight was on her.

"She's not dieting, Maya. Your mother is sick."

"Sick?" Maya clutched her purse to her chest. "How sick?"

"She has pancreatic cancer."

"Cancer?" The words felt like an anchor around her heart, but she managed to ask, "What stage?"

"Stage three. Sophia has been undergoing treatments the last month and, needless to say, it's taken its toll."

"Months? How long have you known about her condition?"

"Maya…"

"How long?" How long had her family had been keeping her in the dark? Why they hadn't told her Sophia was dying?

"Two months."

"And you didn't think to inform me sooner? She's my mother."

"Whom you've been estranged from for five years," Thomas retorted with a huff, "along with the rest of this family."

"You're *not* my family."

"I may not be a blood relation, but I care about Sophia. Raven and I have been carrying the load because her treatments are expensive even with insurance, not to mention the laboratory visits, PET scans and medications. And besides, it's been tearing Raven up seeing Sophia like this and not having anyone to talk to beside me. She needs you."

"She's always *needed* me," Maya responded tightly, "and I've always been there, but what do I get out of it? The short end of the stick."

"I—I thought you were going to let go of the past, Maya. You came today."

Guilt surged through her. Her mother was sick and this wasn't the time or place to take score on who'd harmed who. "Thank you for telling me." She started toward the door.

"What are you going to do?" Thomas inquired.

Maya had no idea. Today had been hard enough as it was. She needed a few minutes to digest everything he'd told her and come up with a plan. "I don't know, but I'll be in touch."

When Maya finally made it back to her hotel room, she was mentally and emotionally exhausted. Confronting the members of her family who'd hurt her and feigning to be the happy aunt had been hard enough. But finding out her mother had cancer was the straw that broke the camel's back. Not only did she have a splitting headache, but her feet were aching from the new designer sandals she'd bought to ensure she measured up to her mother's scrutiny. All she wanted to do was run a hot bath, take some ibuprofen and go to bed. In that exact order.

Maya had kicked off her shoes and was unzipping her dress when there was a knock on her door. She glanced down at her watch. It was seven o'clock. She was in no mood for company after the bomb Thomas dropped on her. And who knew she was in town anyway?

Padding to the door in her bare feet, Maya swung it open in frustration. The person on the other side was someone she never thought she'd see again, not after the one night they'd shared.

"Ayden?"

"Hello, Maya."

Two

At six foot three, weighing about 210 pounds of solid muscle, Ayden looked as yummy as he ever had. Maya was dumbfounded to see the man she'd once adored standing in the flesh in front of her. How could she not be enthralled by those hazel eyes, his strong nose and the light stubble surrounding the best mouth and cleft chin in Texas? He was impeccably dressed in a dark suit with a purple-and-white-striped tie.

"Wh-what are you doing here?" She pulled back her shoulder blades to project that she wasn't taken aback by seeing him after all this time, when she definitely was.

"I came to see you." He rewarded her with one of his sexy smiles. "May I come in?"

"I don't think so…" Maya responded, and began

to close the door. What did you say to the man you'd once slept with, but hadn't seen in five years?

"Maya, please." Ayden stuck a foot in the door to prevent her from shutting it. "I wouldn't have come if it wasn't important."

"All right, but only for a few minutes. It's late and I've had a trying day."

"Thank you." Ayden brushed past Maya, and she caught a hint of his cologne that was so uniquely him. Her stomach clenched in knots like it always did whenever she was around him. And her nipples puckered to attention underneath her dress.

Maya closed the door and turned around to face him. "I repeat, what are you doing here?"

"Is that any way to greet an old friend?" Ayden teased.

Maya folded her arms across her chest because, with Ayden's radar, he might see he'd aroused her, and she'd be mortified if he knew she was still attracted to him. "We were never friends, Ayden."

"Weren't we?" he asked, stepping toward her. "You knew all my secrets. I told you everything."

"And you knew nothing about me."

"That's not true," Ayden said. "I know your favorite color is green. I know *Pretty Woman* is your favorite movie because you're a closet romantic. I know you write in a journal when you think no one is looking. I know you run when you need an outlet to ease tension."

Maya chuckled inwardly. She was surprised he knew that much, but she supposed he would have had to pick up on something. She'd been his executive assistant for half a decade. "All right, you know a few things about me."

Ayden raised a brow. "A few? I think I know a lot more than that."

His implication was clear. He'd known her in the biblical sense and there was no getting around that. But why bring it up? It was over and done with. Finito. He'd made sure of that.

"Why are you here? Clearly, you sought me out. How else would you know I'm back in Austin?"

"I admit I had an investigator try to find you. They informed me you were back for your niece's baptism," Ayden replied. "How did that go? Have you ever been back since…"

He stopped. *Have you ever been back since the night we slept together?* That was the question he couldn't bring himself to finish. At least he had the grace to stop before he embarrassed them both.

"Why would you have an investigator look for me? I don't appreciate you treating me like one of your females," Maya stated.

Ayden was notorious for having the women in his love life investigated to be sure they had no ulterior motives. But Maya, why her? It wasn't like she was one of them. All she'd wanted out of today was to make peace with her family and move on with her life, but now that wasn't possible. First, because of her mother's illness and now Ayden's surprise visit. He wanted something, and despite her anger at his invasion of her privacy she was curious to find out what it was.

"I'm sorry about that, but I didn't know where you were or how to find you. When you left five years ago, you disappeared without a trace."

"Yet, you didn't come looking for me."

"No, I didn't, and I think we both know why. I'm here now and we can talk about that. But first, you mentioned having a bad day. I can't imagine seeing your sister and your ex-boyfriend, now married with a child, was easy, especially when you thought you were headed down the aisle to matrimonial bliss with him yourself."

Maya laughed bitterly to avoid the pain of hearing him say out loud what she'd already thought so many times today. "Apparently, he didn't get the memo, so no, today wasn't a pleasant experience."

Ayden began removing the jacket he was wearing.

"What are you doing?" she asked with a frown. "I didn't ask you to stay. I only agreed to talk for a few minutes." He had no right to make himself comfortable in her hotel room. Not after the way he'd dismissed her so long ago.

Ayden paused. "I'm sorry yet again. I keep apologizing to you tonight." He held up his jacket. "May I?"

"I suppose you can stay a few minutes longer." Ayden draped the jacket across the sofa and sank down into its plushness.

He sat forward on the couch and rested his very large forearms on those powerfully muscled thighs of his. *Jesus!* Why couldn't she think straight when she was around him? Sure, he'd always had this effect on her, but she would have thought his treatment of her five years ago would have cooled any physical response she might have to him now. Apparently, she'd been wrong.

"I'm sorry for what you went through with your sister. It's truly a shame because you're worth a thousand Ravens."

Maya couldn't resist a small smile forming on her lips. Ayden didn't compliment people often. "You don't have to say that."

"You don't think I mean it?"

She spun away and shrugged. It didn't matter. None of it mattered. Ayden, Raven, Thomas—they were all in her rearview. She'd only come back to Austin to get closure and move on with her life. She'd done that. Her mother having cancer had certainly put a wrinkle in her plans to go back to San Antonio and her new life.

When she didn't answer him, Ayden must have risen from the sofa, because Maya felt rather than saw him behind her. "What? What is it that you want from me?"

His large hands grasped her shoulders and guided her around to look at him. "Don't hide from me, Maya. Aren't you tired of it?"

Maya jerked out of his hands. "Don't presume to think you know me, Ayden, just because you can spit out a few obvious facts about me."

"All right. Then how about this. I want you back."

Maya sucked in a deep breath and reminded herself that Ayden was a master at getting his way, especially with women. Over the years, she'd seen him bring the most intelligent and independent women to their knees and have them beg him to take them back. He never did. Instead, he'd have Maya send a farewell gift with his regards. *His regards!*

It must have crushed his ego when she'd chosen not to stay working for him after he bid her adieu after their night together. She wasn't about to go backward even though her heart yearned for more. Still, she was curious and found herself asking, "Why do you want me back?"

"You're the best assistant I ever had. You know how Stewart Investments is run. Hell, how I work. I can count on you to make decisions whether I'm there or not. I trust you implicitly. And remember the Kincaid Corporation deal that I've always wanted a crack at?"

She nodded.

"I have the opportunity to pitch Stewart Investments to them again. You remember how important it was for me to land that account. He's one of my father's largest suppliers. You remember how hard we worked on that first pitch only for him to go to a larger firm. Times have changed and Stewart Investments is in better shape than ever to compete with the big boys."

Ayden didn't want *her* back. He wanted his trusty workaholic assistant back under his grip. "I see."

"You see what?"

"You want me back so I can be your shadow, following you around, being at your beck and call. Well, I'm not your pet, Ayden."

"I never thought you were." He sounded offended. "And I've never treated you like one. You were always a valuable employee."

Maya shook her head. So he was just going to act like it never happened. That they'd never seen each other naked? That they'd hadn't slept together on the bear skin rug in front of his fireplace? "You should go, Ayden." She pushed at his rock-hard chest, which was darn near impenetrable, and walked to the door.

"Why?" He grasped her wrist. His eyes were fire when he said, "You haven't even heard me out."

"Why should I, Ayden, when you refuse to even acknowledge the elephant in the room? I left for a reason and you damn well know why."

Ayden sighed heavily and slowly released her as if she'd struck him. He leaned backward against the door and his intense gaze rested on her. "I'd hoped we wouldn't have to discuss it."

Maya rolled her eyes upward, not wanting him to know how hurt she was by his words. Yet again, Ayden was bruising her already fragile ego. But try as she might, she couldn't ignore the tears that trickled down her cheeks. She wiped at them with the back of her hands.

Ayden swore when he saw her tears. "Christ! I'm sorry, Maya. I didn't mean to hurt you. Not again."

"But yet you continue to do it."

"Not on purpose," Ayden said. "Never on purpose. I care for you, Maya. I always have. I suppose that's why I allowed our relationship to become—" he paused for the right word "—*complicated*. And I take all the blame for what happened. You were destroyed when you came to me, but rather than comforting you, I took advantage of you, and for that I'm terribly sorry. I should never have let things go as far as they did."

Maya glanced up at him through her tears. He was apologizing for making love to her? Was he mad? He was making the situation so much worse, because to her that night had been one of the most sensual encounters she'd ever experienced. But why should she be surprised? He'd only been with her out of pity. He could never find her, Maya Richardson, attractive like he did the many beautiful women he frequently bedded.

Much to her chagrin, Ayden kept going. "The next morning I was so mortified by my actions that I sought to sweep it under the rug like it never happened, which I know wasn't fair to you. But I didn't know what else to do, Maya. Clearly, I'd compromised our working relationship so much that you couldn't come back to work for me. It's why I gave you such a generous termination package. I was sorry for taking advantage of you. I'm still sorry, but I promise, should you choose to work for me again, I will never cross that line and take advantage of you again. I promise I will respect you and your right to have a life of your own without me taking up every minute of your free time."

"Why are you saying all of this?"

"Because I *need* you, Maya. My assistant, Carolyn, is leaving in a couple of months to be a stay-at-home wife and mother, and I need you back."

The desperation in Ayden's tone stunned Maya.

She watched him reach into the jacket pocket of his suit and pull out a thin envelope. He handed it to her. "Read it. I'm offering you an extremely generous salary and benefit package to return to Stewart Investments."

Slowly Maya ripped open the envelope and pulled out the single sheet of paper. The offer letter was nothing short of impressive. The salary was more than generous, it was astronomical. And the benefits of increased 401(k), profit sharing and an abundance of time off was staggering. "Ayden…"

"Listen, I'll make this worth your while. I'm willing to offer you a signing bonus of twenty-five thousand dollars if you'll agree to come back *right now*."

She looked in his direction and saw the worry that she would say no etched all over his face. And she should. She had every right to turn him down. He wasn't good for her. And she'd made a good life in San Antonio. She should go back where it was safe, but when had she ever used her head when it came to this man? The bonus he was offering her was too great a sum to turn down, not when the funds could help her ailing mother. When he looked at her with those puppy-dog eyes, she was a goner.

"Please, don't say no. Think it over."

"I don't need to think it over," she answered impulsively. "My answer is no. I have a life in San Antonio, Ayden. I can't just drop everything because you need me." She had a home, a job she enjoyed and her best friend, Callie. Why would she uproot her life?

"You haven't even thought about it," Ayden said.

"Isn't there anything I can do to entice you? There has to be something."

The thought continued to nag at her that if she accepted Ayden's offer, she could help out with her mother's cancer treatments. Even though they were estranged, Maya couldn't imagine letting her mother suffer when she could have the potential means to help. What kind of person would she be if she did that? But could she go back to working for Ayden knowing her feelings for him weren't truly resolved? "I don't know."

"Maya, we can make this work," Ayden murmured. "With you by my side, we can not only win over Kincaid, but take Stewart Investments to new heights. And with that offer, you would get a share in the earnings. It's a win-win. Please say yes."

"All right, all right, I'll come back."

Ayden couldn't believe the joy that surged through him at Maya's response. Without thinking, he stepped closer. He called himself all kinds of foolish for torturing himself with her familiar sweet aroma, but he couldn't resist. Ayden pulled her into his embrace, squeezing her tightly to him. He felt her breasts pebble against his chest and his groin tightened.

Maya stiffened and Ayden knew he'd done the wrong thing. She didn't welcome his advances. The one night they'd shared had been her attempt to feel loved, coddled, but that was in the past. He mustn't forget that. Still, being in her hotel room was doing funny things to his anatomy again; he pulled away. "I'm sorry. I was just so overjoyed. Won't happen again." He couldn't touch her again. Otherwise, he might lose his head and start to remember what it was like to feel that soft skin of hers as she melted underneath him. He blinked rapidly.

"It's all right," Maya finally said, letting him off the hook. "I guess you were right. It's time I finally stop hiding and return to the life I once loved."

"Do you really mean that?" Ayden quirked a brow. He knew it wasn't entirely true. The report he'd received had told him of Sophia Richardson's health. He knew that the signing bonus was the reason Maya was coming back—she needed it for Sophia Richardson's health costs. He would have given her the money even if she hadn't agreed to come back. Maya was someone he cared about, and if it was in his power to help her mother, he would. He wouldn't want her to experience the guilt he'd felt at not being able to help his mother during her illness. It was guilt he still carried to this day.

"Not the long nights," she added with a smile, "but I did enjoy working with you. We were a good team."

"And we will be again." Once they got back into their work groove, the past would be left behind and they could make a new beginning. He offered Maya his hand. She glanced down at it and Ayden wondered if she was going to renege, but instead her soft fingers clasped his in a firm shake.

"It's a deal."

Ayden grinned. "You don't know how much this means to me."

"Oh, I can guess," Maya laughed. "I suppose there's lots of work piled up?"

Ayden grinned unabashedly. "No. Carolyn is still here for a few weeks, but I wasn't relishing working with someone new. Plus I already had my mind made up that no one but you would do."

Maya Richardson was one of a kind. And although Carolyn had done an acceptable job in her place, Maya was irreplaceable. He'd discovered that when he'd made the mistake of mixing business with pleasure. And speaking of that, it was late. He needed to get out of her room before he did something he couldn't take back. He moved toward the door, but stopped midstep. "How much time do you need to get your affairs in order?"

"A couple of weeks to give notice at my current job. And when I get back to Austin, I'll need some time with Carolyn to get up to speed before she leaves."

He pointed his index finger at her. "I'm holding you to it."

"I've never gone back on my word."

"Very true." She never had and never would, because Maya was a woman he could count on. "I'll see you soon." Ayden left swiftly and closed the door behind him, then leaned up against it.

Closing his eyes, he sucked in a deep breath. It had been dicey in there for a minute. He hadn't realized just how much of a physical tug he'd feel being with Maya again. It had been five years, but the moment she'd opened the door to her hotel room, he'd been transported to that night at his apartment when she'd exploded in his arms and kissed him with a passion unlike anything he'd ever known. Maya had kissed him as if he were a man and not the boss she'd worked with for years. She had aroused him to the point that he'd acted rather than thought about his actions.

For a split second when he'd held her in his arms and their bodies collided, he'd felt compelled to act as he had back then, but in the nick of time he'd managed to do the right thing and move away. He'd just convinced Maya to come back to him and Ayden wasn't about to mess it up because he couldn't keep it in his trousers. He was already the worst kind of scoundrel, having played on feelings he suspected she might still harbor for him.

How did he know?

There had a moment when she thought she'd disguised her true emotions that he had caught a glimpse of something in her eyes. He wasn't positive of how deep her feelings went after all these years, but at the very least, Maya still cared for him, and Ayden had used it to get what he wanted. Which was why he would ensure he kept their relationship platonic going forward—he refused to lose her a second time.

"Are you insane?" Callie stared at Maya in disbelief from across the table of the Starbucks where they'd met the following afternoon when she returned to San Antonio.

"No, I'm not."

"Clearly, you must have lost your mind." Callie

reached across the short distance to place the back of her hand on Maya's forehead. "Why else would you agree to go back and work for Ayden?"

"He made me an attractive offer."

"This isn't about money, Maya," Callie responded hotly, "and you know it. You're going because you're still hung up on the man."

"That's not true."

Callie raised a brow.

"It's not. Listen, Callie, I got over Ayden a long time ago, when he nearly kicked me out of his place the morning after we had sex. It made me wise up real quick."

"Well, if that's the case, why go back for more? Why put yourself in harm's way? You know you're not immune to his charms. And I suspect he knows. How else would he have lured you back into his web?"

"I'm not his prey."

"Are you sure about that?" Callie inquired, sipping on her Frappuccino. "Because I suspect you have no idea what you're in for. Five years ago, you opened Pandora's box and found out what it was like to *be* with the man. Do you honestly think you can act as if those feelings never existed?"

"He's offering me enough money to ensure I ignore them."

"I still don't understand, after the way he treated you."

Maya leaned back in her chair and regarded her best friend. She hadn't yet divulged her mother's condition. "Mama is ill."

"Excuse me?"

"Thomas shared with me that she has pancreatic cancer."

"Omigod!" Callie jerked back in her seat. Then she immediately reached across the table and clutched Maya's hand. "What's the diagnosis?"

"They are hoping that, after chemo and radiation, she will go into remission, but the treatments are expensive. Thomas and Raven have been helping out, but with the baby, they are stretched thin."

Callie nodded. "Now I understand why you accepted Ayden's offer."

"The influx of cash will help Mama. Without worrying about finances, she can focus on getting better." Although she and her mother had never seen eye to eye, she was *her mother*. How could she not help out?

"Oh, Maya." Callie's eyes filled with tears. "You are so selfless. Does your mother have any idea of your plans?"

"I called her earlier and told her I was moving back to Austin," Maya replied. "She was pleased that I would be closer, but I didn't tell her about the money. She knows Raven and Thomas have been covering the out-of-pocket expenses, but I don't want her to know that I'll take up the slack going forward. "And promise me you won't tell her."

"Of course not. I would never betray your confidence. But where are you going to live? With your mother? I can't imagine you staying with your sister."

"That's completely out of the question. Although I'm willing to get to know my niece and I accepted

Raven's apology, it's going to be a long time, if ever, before we can get back to the sister relationship we once shared. And as for my mother, we're like oil and water. We don't mix. If I stayed with her, all she would do is criticize and compare me to Raven like she did when we were children. It is best if I find my own place, but I'll visit Mom." She'd contacted a property management company who'd forwarded some listings for sublets and short-term rentals until she could find a place she liked.

"All right. I just worry about you, and not only with where you lay your head. I'm talking about Ayden. You're walking into the lion's den with no protection for your heart."

"My heart has nothing to do with the situation. What I felt for Ayden is in the past."

"That's easy to say when you're not seeing the man day and night. I remember the hours you kept before."

"It won't be like that now. He promised. Plus, he didn't want me five years ago, so nothing has really changed."

"Maya...you were intimate with Ayden. Trust me, he *wanted* you."

"For all of five seconds. Anyway, have a little faith in me, Callie. I can do this. I *have* to. Not for myself, but for Mama."

Three

Two weeks later, Maya sat outside her mother's house with the engine of her Honda running. She'd arrived in Austin the day before. Ayden had ensured her sign-on bonus check had arrived within days of accepting his offer, so she'd been able to secure her short-term rental for next six months. She'd put most of her belongings in storage until she was sure returning to Stewart Investments would work out. In the meantime, she'd kept the news of her return to Austin a secret from her family, but now it was time to face the music. Since her relationship with her sister was strained, she'd informed Raven via text of her plans a few days ago. Raven was happy she was coming back home if the emoji that accompanied her texts were anything to go by, but Maya hadn't yet told her mother.

After turning off the ignition, Maya exited the car and climbed the porch steps. The neighborhood looked much the same as it had when she'd left some ten-odd years ago except now the homes appeared older and more worn. Her mother's could use a coat of paint and the lawn needed mowing. Maya was just about to ring the doorbell when the door swung wide.

"Maya?" her mother said incredulously.

"Yes, it's me. Can I come in?" Maya was startled by how thin her mother was. Although it had only been a little over two weeks since she'd last seen her, Sophia had lost another five pounds. Her normally dark hair lay limp on her shoulders and the simple print house shift she was wearing hung off her slender frame. Meanwhile her skin seemed sallow and her eyes had sunk even deeper into her face.

"Of course." Sophia stood back and motioned her into the formal living room. "Would you like anything to drink? I think I have some sweet tea in the fridge."

Maya shook her head. "Nothing for me." She didn't plan on staying long.

Her mother took a seat on the sofa and Maya did the same. "What are you doing here? I thought you went back to San Antonio."

"I did, but I came back."

"So you could start to mend fences with your sister?" her mother offered, folding one leg over the other.

One day, yes, but not now." Although she'd accepted Raven's marriage and her baby niece, Maya wasn't ready to tackle more than that. She had Ayden to deal with.

"Oh, Maya. That's water under the bridge now. You have to let it go and move on."

"I have let it go, Mother," Maya responded. "I came to the baptism."

"Yes, you did. And that was a start."

"Listen, Mama. I didn't come here to talk about Raven. I came to let you know that I'm moving back home. I've gotten my old position back at Stewart Investments."

"With that good-looking fella you used to work for?" Sophia touched her chest. "Now there was a sight for sore eyes if ever I saw one. That man is gorgeous. Why couldn't you ever snag him?"

Of course her mother would think along those lines. But finding a man wasn't a number-one priority for Maya. She was an independent woman who used her brains to get ahead. "Ayden is my boss, nothing more." And there could never been anything ever again.

"That's too bad. With his looks and all that money, you'd never have to worry a day in your life about how to pay the next bill."

"That's the thing, Mama. I make good money and I can more than help out with whatever it is that you need around the house." Maya looked about the room and noted the peeling wallpaper and loose wood flooring.

Her mother rose to her feet and began pacing the room. "I don't need your handouts, Maya Richardson. I've been doing just fine without you. Raven and Thomas have seen to that."

"I'm sure they have. I just thought—" Her mother might want her help? It was clear Sophia didn't want Maya to know about her cancer.

"That you could come in on your white horse and save the day?" Sophia interrupted. "Well, that's not necessary. We've got it covered."

Maya sighed. "Very well, then." She would just have to tackle her mother's financial woes a different way. She pulled out a slip of paper. "Here's my new address and phone number if you need to reach me since it's clear you're doing just fine without me."

She rose to her feet to depart, but her mother touched her arm softly.

"I'm sorry, Maya. That came out all wrong. I'm glad you're back in town and that you took the time to come see me," she said. "I just don't want to be anyone's charity case, ya hear?"

"Yes, ma'am." Maya nodded and allowed Sophia to walk her to the front door. "I'll stop by again real soon."

"I'd like that."

Maya let out a deep breath once the door closed behind her. What had she expected, that her mother would welcome her with open arms? She and Sophia had never had that kind of mother-daughter relationship. Raven was her favorite child and that hadn't changed. Thanks to her therapy, Maya had learned to accept it and to understand her mother loved her in her own way even though she had a funny way of showing it. But it didn't matter. Maya would figure out a way to help with Sophia's medical bills despite her stubbornness. If there was a will, there was a way.

The next morning, Maya wasn't nervous as she walked through the revolving doors of Stewart Investments' offices. She strutted toward the elevator bank feeling great. She was returning to her old stomping grounds and it felt like home.

She planned on spending the next week gathering as much information from Carolyn as possible. She was so busy running through a mental checklist that she didn't notice Ayden until he was standing beside her.

"Good morning, Maya."

Maya popped her head up and looked at him. "Good morning." She glanced down at her watch. "You're here a bit early, aren't you?" It was a little after seven, and typically Ayden came in around eight. First, he hit the gym for a morning workout before having two cups of strong black coffee for breakfast. Sometimes with fruit and dry toast, other times with an egg-white omelet. She still knew his schedule like the back of her hand.

A chime echoed in the lobby and the elevator doors opened. "Times have changed," Ayden said as they entered. "Since I didn't have you, I've had to adjust."

"And you will need to adjust again because I like having the morning to myself."

Ayden chuckled. "And now so do I."

Maya wondered if she would have time to mentally

prepare for working with him again? Apparently not, because here she was being thrown into the deep end of the ocean without a life vest.

They were both silent on the ride to the fiftieth floor. When they reached the top, Maya exited the elevator first. Ayden fell into step beside her as they walked toward the executive offices.

"Not much has changed," Ayden said, "except some of the decor."

The interior offices that were once browns and beige had been replaced with an open concept done in whites and primary colors. The new atmosphere was bright and airy. "I like it."

"I'm glad. I want you to love your working environment since you'll be spending a great deal of time here."

"You promised me that would change," Maya responded.

"I did," Ayden said, glancing down at her. "And I will hold up my end of the bargain."

Despite what she'd told Callie, Maya doubted he would be able to help himself. Some days there would be long hours, but she wouldn't let it consume her life as it once had.

When they made it to the area outside Ayden's office, she placed her purse on what was once her desk and studied her surroundings. It felt surreal being back after all this time.

"Everything all right?" Ayden inquired from behind her.

Maya whirled around. "Yes, of course."

"You can change anything you like."

"Wow! I'm not even out the door and you're ready to replace all semblance of me?" a beautiful blonde said as she walked toward them. She wore a chic knee-length black sheath and to-die-for designer pumps. She was nearly as tall as Ayden. "Hey, it's not my fault you want to leave the best job in town to go off and play wife and mom," Ayden said.

Maya could only assume the stunning Scandinavian beauty was none other than Carolyn, Ayden's current assistant. She stepped forward and held out her hand. "Maya. Maya Richardson."

Carolyn shook her hand. "Ah, Maya. I've heard a lot of great things about you. It's a pleasure to finally meet you."

"Congratulations on your pregnancy." Maya tried not to let the envy show on her face that yet another woman was living the life she'd always wanted while she was destined to remain alone.

"It doesn't mean I'm not here for both of you," she said, looking at Maya. "I'm just a phone call away if you need me."

"Hopefully, that won't be necessary if you get me up to speed this week."

"Let's get started." Carolyn made for her desk.

"I'll leave you to it." Ayden disappeared into his office and closed the door.

Carolyn chuckled to herself. "He's not much of talker, is he?"

"Nope. Never has been and never will be."

"I hear you." Carolyn stashed her purse in her

drawer and locked it before taking a seat at her desk. "When I first started working here, it took him months to learn my name. I guess he'd gone through so many assistants he couldn't keep up. Eventually, I put my foot down and forced him to acknowledge me. We've gotten along marvelously ever since."

"That's great."

"It wasn't easy filling your shoes," Carolyn continued as she turned on her laptop and punched in the appropriate password. "Ayden thought the world of you and made sure everyone knew it."

"Did he really?" Maya was surprised.

Years ago, she'd learned there were only two avenues a girl could go. The pretty route or the smart route. Her mother had always told Maya her looks were unremarkable, so she'd become a bookworm and excelled in her studies. After college, she'd had options, but had been afraid to branch out. Needing work, she'd become a temporary admin and found she was skilled at multitasking for successful men. That was how she'd come to work for Ayden. Her reputation as the miracle worker had wowed him. It was good to know that her unwavering work ethic had garnered his respect.

Maya spent the duration of the morning going through the dozens of active client files to help her become familiar with all the players. It was well past noon when she looked up from the table in the small breakout conference room she'd relegated herself to and found Carolyn at the doorway.

"You hungry yet?" Carolyn asked. "Because I'm

starved. Eating for two has me ravenous all the time."
She patted her small baby bump.

"You go ahead. I'm just finishing up and will grab
a quick bite later."

Finally she stopped long enough to grab a salad
from the building's café only to return to the mountain of paper. Hours later, Carolyn stopped by to tell
her she was leaving for the day. Maya hadn't realized
it was so late, but she waved goodbye.

She was reading her last file when she felt Ayden's
presence. Heat washed over Maya at seeing him again.
He'd abandoned his jacket and tie, and had rolled up
his sleeves to reveal enormous biceps. Ayden came
closer and Maya could swear she felt a light spark inside her when he looked at her so intently.

"Burning the midnight oil?"

"Excuse me?"

He tapped his watch. "It's after six. I thought we
agreed that you would have a life outside of this office."

Maya pinched the bridge of her nose. "Well, I intend to. I just finished the last file." She closed the
folder and placed it on the table. "Guess I should get
on home, or should I say to my short-term rental."
She wasn't ready to sign a long-term lease just yet;
the rental was affordable and allowed her the flex-
ibility to move quickly if working with Ayden again
didn't pan out.

"How about dinner?" Ayden asked, jamming his
hands into his trouser pockets. How was it he could

look so amazingly good with several days' worth of stubble on his jaw?

"Not necessary. I can pick up some takeout on the way home."

He studied her through hooded eyes. "I wasn't trying anything, Maya. I just thought after a long first day, it might be nice to catch up. And it's not like we haven't shared a meal together before."

He was right, of course. They'd worked late and eaten together on many occasions, though usually it had been takeout, not a formal dinner. But how bad could it be? "All right, I'd like that."

"Let me grab my jacket and I'll be right with you." He was gone for several seconds, giving Maya enough time to regret accepting the invitation. Why was she doing this to herself? Was she so determined to prove that he had no power over her that she would agree to be alone with him? Maybe she was. If they were going to work together, Maya would have to be comfortable spending time in his company. *Alone.*

Dinner on the terrace at the quaint Italian restaurant was exactly that. Ayden didn't make any untoward moves. Instead, he was nothing short of hospitable and caring, holding out her chair, making sure he selected her favorite wine and generally steering the conversation to lighter topics such as movies, books and his favorite sports team. Maya began to relax.

Ayden could be great company. She found herself laughing at his anecdotes and funny jokes. She recalled how he had a sense of humor, but it had taken time to manifest itself. Back in the day, he'd close his door for hours, shutting himself off from the world, only calling Maya on the intercom to do his bidding. In time, Ayden had learned to open up to her and share some of his past, his struggles and his hopes for Stewart Investments. It's why she knew how important securing Kincaid's business was to him. He was more approachable than he'd ever been, and Maya had to admit she liked this new version of Ayden. Perhaps she'd had something to do with him learning to be more open.

When the dessert menu came along, Maya patted her full stomach. "I don't think so."

"C'mon, don't be a spoilsport. Their cannoli is the best."

"Sounds like you know from personal experience?"

"I do." Ayden turned to the waitress, who was still standing near their table. "We'll have the cannoli and coffee."

"Sure thing, Mr. Stewart," the waitress replied, and scurried away.

"This was really nice, Ayden. Thank you."

"You're welcome. I told you things were going to be different this time."

"Yes, you did," Maya replied, "but I wasn't sure."

"I've learned from the past and generally don't make the same mistakes over again."

Maya wondered if that meant becoming intimate with her. She would never know because the waitress returned with their dessert and coffee. Maya watched Ayden pour them each a cup and was surprised when he put three cubes of sugar and a splash of milk in hers. "Thanks." When had he learned how she liked her coffee? Probably the same time he'd discovered she liked to run and kept a journal.

"No problem."

Soon dessert was over and Ayden was walking Maya to her Honda. "Thank you for dinner."

"You're welcome. It's the least I could do since you're working so hard."

"I worked late so I could get up to speed."

"Well, I want you to know I appreciate it. It's good to have you back, Maya. I missed you."

He missed her.

"I missed you, too." Maya didn't wait for his response, and wasted no time hopping into her car and speeding away. She needed distance.

Once she had made it to her apartment, Maya tried not to think about Ayden. She had to focus on something else, anything else, so she called Raven. After her mother's refusal of her help, Maya was going to have to find another approach.

Raven answered on the second ring. "Maya, it's so good to hear from you. Have you made it safely to Austin from San Antonio?"

"I have," Maya replied, "but this really isn't a social call."

"Oh, all right. What's going on?"

Maya heard the disappointment in her sister's voice, but she pressed on. The familial relationship they'd once shared had been shattered. "Thomas told me about Mama's medical bills."

"Really? When did you speak with him?"

"After the baptism, but that's beside the point. I want to help out with the house bills and Mama doesn't want me to. When I mentioned it, she told me you and Thomas had it under control."

"I wish that were true, but with a new baby, it's gotten tight paying for her medications, plus the balance the insurance doesn't cover. Any help you could give would be greatly appreciated."

"Well, I'm here now. Tell me what I can do."

Their call ended soon after, with Raven promising to email Maya with the details of what was outstanding and any upcoming payments. Maya had set aside a good portion of her $25,000 bonus for her mother's care. Feeling accomplished, she retired to bed, but when she did, her mind wandered to Ayden's words. He missed her. She told herself he missed the dependable, efficient assistant who could keep him on task. She knew her job and how to effectively implement the decisions he made. Ayden was no more interested in her than he'd been five years ago. At least now he valued her and liked her well enough to offer friendship. And that was sufficient, because quite frankly she had as much as she could handle on her plate. She was trying to reconnect with her mother while she still had the chance. And maybe she'd even try her hand at dating again. Maya was determined to take back her life, starting now.

Four

The next morning, Maya arrived at the office around the same time as she had the previous day. Neither Ayden nor Carolyn were in sight this time. Maya set about turning on the Keurig machine and making herself a cup of coffee. Although she'd slept through the night, she still felt tired. Probably because it wasn't her own bed in San Antonio.

Wouldn't it be nice if she were sharing it with a certain CEO?

Maya tried to shake the cobwebs from her brain. Why were thoughts of Ayden popping into her head? She'd stopped fantasizing about him years ago. Why was this happening again? Was her subconscious trying to tell her that she wasn't as over him as she thought?

She was heading back to her desk when Carolyn's phone rang. She glanced at her watch. It was early for the phones to start ringing. Maya picked up the receiver. "Stewart Investments."

"Maya, it's Carolyn."

"Carolyn? Is everything okay?" Her voice sounded weak, as if she'd been crying.

"N-no, it's not. I woke up this morning and I was spotting. My husband took me the hospital and we are waiting to see the doctor. Oh, Maya, I don't want to lose this baby."

"And you won't." Maya tried to sound encouraging. "You're a strong, healthy woman, Carolyn. You can do this."

"I hope so, but Ayden…"

"I'll take care of him, don't you worry. You just take care of yourself and that baby."

"Thank you, I appreciate it. But you should know he has a big meeting coming up tonight with a high-profile client. I finished the presentation yesterday. It will just need to be printed out and bound."

"I'm on it. Don't worry. I've got this. If you can, call me later and let me know you're okay?"

"I will. And Maya?"

"Yes?"

"Thank you."

The line went dead and Maya stared at the receiver in her hand. That was how Ayden found her as he approached. "Maya?" He dropped his briefcase and rushed toward her. "Is everything okay?"

She nodded. "Yes, yes, I'm fine. It's not me. It's

Carolyn. She's in the hospital. Could be something wrong with the baby."

"Oh, Lord!"

"I know, right?" Tears formed in the corners of Maya's eyes at the thought that Carolyn could lose the baby. Although she'd only just met her, it was obvious how much she wanted to be a mother.

Ayden crouched by the desk and reached for Maya's hands. "We have to believe that she and the baby will be all right."

Maya nodded and slowly Ayden released her hands to stand up straight. "She told me about a dinner meeting you have tonight with the Kincaid's. That's great. I know how much you've wanted their business."

"Yes, Carolyn was working up a prospectus."

"I'll have it ready for you."

"You mean, ready for us."

Maya stared back in confusion. "I don't understand."

"Carolyn was accompanying me to this dinner tonight. Kincaid is big on family. Although I don't have one to speak of, Carolyn was going to pinch-hit as my plus one. Can you do the same?"

"I suppose."

His brow furrowed and he paused. "Will that be a problem?"

Dinner again with Ayden, except this time she would be his plus one? The evening prior she'd been able to justify it as two people sharing a meal after working late, but this felt different. Maya had to remind herself that this was business. Like Carolyn, she was attending to help him pitch Stewart Investments to his dream client. "No, it won't be a problem."

She hit the ground running the rest of day, working through all the emails, answering those that were urgent and forwarding those requiring Ayden's input. She set up a spreadsheet for his active deals that she'd studied up on yesterday. And thank God she had.

Later that day, Maya wanted to breathe a sigh of relief but fretted over what to wear. Having let her go an hour early to freshen up, Ayden planned on picking her up at 7:00 p.m. and she still hadn't selected a dress. Most of her clothing was still in storage, so her options were severely limited. Maya settled on a one-shoulder body-con dress. Callie had convinced Maya that with her slender figure she could pull it off. It wasn't like she had a lot of opportunities to dress up. Her life in San Antonio had been rather boring up to this point. At least the dress would hug the few curves she had. After adding some chandelier earrings, a spritz of perfume, and some mascara, blush and lipstick, she was ready.

Ayden was already in the lobby speaking with the security guard, which allowed Maya time to survey him. It was impossible to stop herself from staring at him like some love-struck teenager. He was powerfully built, and his suit fitted his broad frame like no other man she'd ever known. Maya felt breathless and her stomach was tied in knots. Ayden had the looks to go with his physique. Those stunning hazel-gray eyes, perpetual five-o'clock shadow and chiseled cheekbones caused her to suck in a deep calming breath.

The truth was, she could have kept looking at him forever, but as if sensing he was being watched, Ayden glanced up and his eyes fastened on hers. He shook the man's hand and walked toward her. Maya's heart rate began galloping at an alarming speed. Her mouth suddenly felt as dry as the Sahara Desert, but she managed, "I'm ready."

Ayden trapped her with his eyes. Helplessly she gazed up into those murky depths, which had suddenly darkened from hazel to something more mysterious. Maya's entire body burned from the look he was giving her. Then he blinked and it was gone, and Maya wondered if she'd imagined the lust she was almost certain was there.

Ayden offered Maya his arm and she took it. "Let's go."

They rode to the restaurant in companionable silence. Neither of them seemed too keen on talking until both their cell phones buzzed, indicating a text message. Maya pulled hers from her clutch. It was Carolyn. "She and the baby are okay," Maya said, turning to Ayden.

He glanced up from the road to reward her with a smile. "That's wonderful news. I'm glad to hear it."

The phone buzzed again and Maya quickly read the message. "But she's not returning to the office. The doctor has indicated her pregnancy is high risk and is putting her on bed rest."

"That's a shame because it leaves you in quite the lurch."

"Not really," Maya said. "I'm more than capable of

stepping in, picking up the baton and running with it. I'm just glad I spent yesterday poring through those files."

"So am I, Maya. So am I."

When they made it to the restaurant, the hostess sat them at a table already occupied by Ayden's prospective client. "Mr. Kincaid. Ryan," Ayden said. He offered the elder Kincaid and his son handshakes. "Pleasure to see you both. And is this your lovely wife?"

"Yes, it is." The older man beamed with pride. "Sandy, I'd like you to meet Ayden Stewart…" The petite brunette rose from her seat and Ayden shook her hand.

"Nice to meet you."

"And of course, you know my son. Ryan, Ayden is the man who's going to make us millions."

"Mr. Stewart," Ryan replied, "my father thinks very highly of you. I'm curious to hear what ideas you have for us."

"Of course, but please let me introduce Maya Richardson." Ayden slid his hand to the small of her back and edged her over to the group.

"Ms. Richardson." Mr. Kincaid leaned over and clasped her hand. "You're looking quite lovely this evening. Isn't she, Ayden?"

Ayden's eyes glowed with fire when he looked at her, and Maya felt her belly clench in response. "She is."

"I agree with you, Father," Ryan commented, and Maya's heart started in her chest. There was naked interest in the younger Kincaid's eyes as he searched her face. She wasn't used to being the center of attention, especially from such a good-looking man with his tanned skin, shock of dark hair and stunning blue eyes.

Ayden reached for her then, tugging her forward. A sharp streak of sensation coursed through Maya at his touch. She nearly stumbled into the chair he'd pulled out for her.

Ryan reached for her to assist, but Ayden glanced up at him and said, "I've got her."

"Thank you." Maya hoped her blush wasn't showing at having both men so clearly interested in her well-being. Not that there was any competition. Her nerves had been shot the moment she'd seen Ayden in the lobby. She'd known it was going to be difficult working for Ayden again, but she hadn't realized that she would be thrown into a situation so quickly, especially when she still harbored residual feelings for him.

Before she could even gather herself, she felt the warm strength of Ayden's hand as he patted her thigh, probably in an effort to ease the tension that was no doubt radiating off her. His touch was oddly comforting, even though it made her tingle and brought her entire body to life. A tight coil formed in her tummy and was quickly racing upward toward her breasts, making them feel fuller, heavier. Maya willed her wayward body to relax. She grabbed her water glass and drank generously, hoping the chilled water would cool off her hot flesh.

"So how long have you two been seeing each other?" Mr. Kincaid inquired.

"It's not like that," Ayden quickly responded. "Maya is my assistant. She often entertains clients with me."

Mr. Kincaid wasn't fazed. "My wife was my secretary, too, and as you can see that didn't stop us."

"So you're single?" Ryan's question lingered in the air.

"Um, yes, I am." Maya offered Ryan a small smile.

"It's good to know there's hope for the rest of us mortals," Ryan said.

Was he trying to flirt with her? Because she'd never dated outside her race. She was woefully out of practice in the dating department. It was safer to change the topic. And she did. She discovered that the Kincaids had been married for thirty years and had a daughter, as well.

"Family is very important to me," Mr. Kincaid said. "Stewart Investments is one of the top investment firms in Texas, but it isn't all about money. I want to find someone who values family above the almighty dollar. I used to be all-business in the past and it nearly cost me my wife." He looked at Mrs. Kincaid. "That's why it's so important to work with people who are well-rounded and have work-life balance because, although I enjoy my money, I don't want to be consumed by it, or by the quest to make more. Tell me about your family, Ayden? Are you related to Henry Stewart of Stewart Technologies?"

Maya felt Ayden stiffen at her side, and everyone,

including Ryan, seemed to be rapt waiting for his answer. She knew how much Ayden hated talking about his family, much less the father who'd never acknowledged him. It was a touchy subject and one she knew he didn't want to discuss with strangers. The only reason she happened to learn of the connection was because when his mother passed away, an arrangement had arrived from Stewart Technologies.

"He's my father, but we're estranged," Ayden said finally, after several long, tense moments. "I was very close with my mother, but she died about five years ago, so I'm in short supply on family."

"I'm sorry to hear that," Mr. Kincaid said.

Ayden nodded, but Maya couldn't let it go at that. "You won't find another investment firm that is more dedicated, honest and forthcoming than Stewart Investments. Clients are more than just numbers or facts and figures on a spreadsheet, Mr. Kincaid. Ayden cares about you and your family's future and wants what's best to grow your portfolio."

Mr. Kincaid turned to Ayden. "You've got quite the advocate sitting next to you."

Ayden turned to look at Maya. "Don't I know it."

Ayden was stunned by Maya's impassioned speech on his behalf. He'd never had someone have his back, except maybe Luke, and he was an ocean away. He'd always known that Maya was one in a million, but it was more than that. She was a truly exceptional person, and he doubted he'd truly realized just how exceptional up until this moment.

"You have quite the *assistant*," Mr. Kincaid added. Ayden caught his emphasis on the word *assistant*, because she certainly wasn't acting like one.

"Yes, I know." When he'd arrived in the lobby of her apartment, he'd been unable to mask the unadulterated lust that surged through him at seeing her in the slinky red dress. He'd never even seen Maya in color. She usually wore black, navy and beige, but then again, he hadn't seen her in five years. He was supposed to be keeping his distance and maintaining a professional decorum with Maya, but how was he supposed to when she looked sinfully sexy?

The dress showed off her long legs and incredibly fit physique. Running had done her body good. She was tall, graceful and perfectly proportioned. She had long legs, a waist that he could easily span with his hands and two round orbs for breasts. She had an understated beauty and Ayden was having a hard time ignoring her, as evidenced by the tightening of his body. He didn't need this now. Not when his energies had to be focused on securing Kincaid's business. And that wasn't the only problem: Ryan was making no attempt to hide his interest in Maya, and Ayden didn't like it one bit. He reached for his wineglass and drank liberally.

So he switched gears, charming the Kincaids well into the third course. Maya and Mrs. Kincaid were chatting quietly in the dining room about God knows what while he, Ryan and Mr. Kincaid had retired to the cigar room, so Kincaid could try one of the restaurant's Cubans they were known for. Ayden didn't care for cigars, so he opted for an aged cognac.

"There's nothing better than a fine cigar," Mr. Kincaid said, puffing on his cigar.

"I hear they are some of the best in town," Ayden said, and sipped on his drink.

"Speaking of the best...that assistant of yours," Mr. Kincaid responded. "She's a treasure, that girl."

"Yes, she is. And to be frank, I lost her some years back because I didn't appreciate what I had. I don't intend to make that mistake again."

"Is that right?" Ryan smirked. Ayden could see Ryan's mind working on whether that gave him an edge with Maya. It didn't. Maya was *his*. Well, not his, per se, but she was off-limits to the younger Kincaid.

Mr. Kincaid turned to him. "I appreciate a man who can admit he made a mistake and not let pride come before a fall."

By the end of the evening, Ayden was shaking hands with the Kincaids and wishing them a good night as he sent them back in a limousine to their hotel. Meanwhile, out the corner of his eye, he could see Ryan speaking privately with Maya. He saw him hand her a business card and watched Maya give him a smile. Then Ryan touched her arm as he left. Ayden was not amused. He was thankful when Ryan got in the limo and they drove away. He handed the valet his ticket.

"That went rather well," Maya said. "Don't you think?"

Ayden gave a half smile. "Yes, it did. Thanks to you."

"Me?" Her voice rose an octave. "I didn't do anything."

"Of course you did. You had the Kincaids, each and every one of them, eating out the palm of your hand. I'm impressed and so glad I brought you along."

Maya shrugged and smiled smugly. "What can I say? We make a good team."

Ayden met her gaze. Their eyes locked, held. "Yes, we do."

Desire flared, hot and tangible, between them. Ayden didn't know what possessed him, but he stepped right into her personal space. He wished she hadn't looked at him like that. It heated his blood, and the cool air did little to settle the fever that was coursing through him. He caught her hand and pulled her toward him, compelled to do what he'd wanted to do all night, which was kiss her. He didn't know where this wildness was coming from because he was usually so composed, but Maya's proximity throughout the evening had gotten to him. Her eyes sparked and flared, radiating heat right through him. When she wet her lips with her tongue, Ayden found himself wondering what she would taste like again.

He was bending his head to brush his lips across hers when the valet pulled up in Ayden's Bentley, breaking the trance. He'd been just as enthralled by Maya as Ryan had been, perhaps more so because he knew her, had *been* with her. But he couldn't be again. He'd given her his word.

Slowly Ayden released her. He gave Maya a small smile because in her eyes he could see she'd been anticipating that kiss as much as he'd been. Would it have been light and sweet, or would it have been the frantic passion they'd shared so long ago?

They would never know because Ayden quickly moved to open the passenger door. Maya didn't say a word for several moments. She simply stared at him in confusion. He knew he'd given her mixed signals. One minute he was hot for her and the next he was pushing her away. But it was for the best. When he didn't say a word, Maya finally stepped toward the car and slid in. When she did, the skirt of her dress hiked up and Ayden couldn't resist feasting his eyes on her sumptuous thighs.

When he glanced up, Ayden found Maya watching him. Had she known where his thoughts had gone? If so, her eyes were shuttered and she didn't let on. He closed the door, came around to the driver's side and jumped in. After buckling up, he pulled away from the curb.

The drive to her apartment was fraught with pent-up tension. Awareness rippled through the air, but Ayden ignored it. He had to take Maya back home while he still could. He just couldn't walk her up-stairs, because if he did, he'd be asking to come in-side. In more ways than one.

They pulled up to the apartment's main entrance ten minutes later. He glanced at Maya. "Thanks for tonight. You did great. Sleep well."

She didn't even look at him as she said tersely,

"Good night." Seconds later, she was out of the car without a backward glance. He stared at her retreating figure before pulling away to drive home.

Could he blame her for being angry at him?

He'd behaved horribly earlier, pulling her to him like he was going to start something he couldn't possibly finish. But Maya had been different tonight. He'd seen another side to her. A sexy siren. And it was contrary to what he'd always known about her. That mix had desire ripping through him, igniting a fierce desire to kiss her, claim what had once been his. Because there was no way Ryan Kincaid was going to have his woman. But did he really have a right to think this way? Wasn't this what had led him down the wrong path and caused Maya to leave in the first place? It had taken months to find the right person to replace her, and although Carolyn was awesome, she couldn't read his mind like Maya. He had to back off.

It was simply that talking and laughing with her tonight had caused memories to resurface. There were sparks of desire between them, of that there was no doubt. He would love nothing better than to kiss her, touch her and undress her. But there was no way he would or could allow them to burn as hot as they once had.

Maya had made it very clear that she wasn't interested in rekindling a personal relationship with him. And he had to respect her decision even if his libido didn't like it. And truth be told, she was too good for him anyway. She certainly wouldn't settle for a light and sexual affair, which was all Ayden was capable of. Maya was the kind of woman that you married and made the mother of your children. Ayden wanted no part of that life, and his penance was to go to bed longing for a woman he could never have.

Five

Maya was furious as she stormed through the apartment lobby toward the elevators. How dare he touch her like that? Look at her like that? Who the hell did Ayden think he was? Once again, he was showing that he could not be trusted. He'd told her that their relationship, going forward, would be strictly business, but tonight he'd changed the rules. Back at the restaurant, he'd pulled her to him, like...well, like he wanted her. Her stomach had lit up like a ball of fire, and she'd sparked at the desire that had lurked in those hazel-gray depths. Then, just as quickly, he'd cast her aside as if it hadn't happened.

Just as he had five years ago.

The elevator chimed and Maya entered. Leaning against the wall, she exhaled and closed her eyes. She was trying to force the kick of adrenaline she'd experienced to dissipate. Why had he done it? Stirred up a hornet's nest of emotions that she'd kept buried? For so long, she'd accepted that Ayden didn't want her. Never had. That he'd slept with her that night out of pity. And then tonight, he'd flipped the script, making her wonder if she'd gotten it wrong all those years ago. Had he wanted to make love to her? Had it been more to him? Is that what had scared him off?

No, no, no. She shook her head. She couldn't do this to herself. She'd dealt with this years ago. She couldn't resurrect those feelings of self-doubt. Not again. Maya had gone to therapy to deal with Raven and Thomas's betrayal and her night with Ayden. It had all done a number on her ego and self-confidence, but she'd picked up the pieces and finally felt as if she'd let go of the past. She'd faced those demons a few weeks ago when she'd gone to her niece's baptism.

Maya had hoped that taking this job again would not only help her mother financially, but exorcise those buried demons and remind her of her self-worth. She didn't need Ayden's mixed signals and she wouldn't abide it. Not anymore. She wouldn't just accept what Ayden or anyone else doled out to her. He would soon learn that she'd grown and was no longer a doormat.

The next morning, Maya arrived at the office ready to work and full of spice. She was prepared to give Ayden a piece of her mind, but he called to let her know that he had morning meetings and wouldn't be in until later. Maya was puzzled. There were no appointments on his calendar, so she could only assume he didn't want to face her. And perhaps it was for the best. Now she would have time to cool down and regain her composure.

By the time Ayden arrived midmorning, Maya had determined to put last night in the past, like an aberration, and move forward with the job. When he strolled into the office, walking with a lithe, purposeful gait, threading his way toward Maya, she was in control.

And so was Ayden.

"Maya—" he thrust a sheath of papers across her desk without looking in her direction "—I need copies of these immediately." He swept past her into his office and closed the door.

It didn't surprise her that he was ignoring what had transpired last night. He was good at that, acting as if nothing had happened. She would do the same. She did as instructed and made the copies. When she was done, she knocked on his office door. A terse "come in" was issued and she entered.

Ayden's office was as immaculate as the man himself. It held a dark walnut desk along with built-in bookshelves that spanned an entire wall. A sitting area with a leather sofa, low table and wet bar was in the opposite corner.

She headed to his desk. "Here you are." She leaned over to hand him the papers, but he seemed determined to act as if whatever he was reviewing on his laptop was more important than acknowledging her.

So Maya dropped the copies with a flop on his laptop. That got his attention and he glanced up.

"Is there anything else, *boss*?" She said the last word with a measure of sarcasm, impossible to ignore.

His brow rose. "Actually, yes. Can you get Kincaid on the line?"

"I'll get right on that." Seconds later, she was slamming his door and returning to her desk. The jerk!

She was smarting over his casual disregard when a delivery man strolled toward her with one of the biggest bouquets of flowers Maya had ever seen. "Maya Richardson?" he inquired.

"Yes, that's me."

"These are for you. Sign here, please." He handed her a clipboard while he placed the fragrant bouquet on her desk. Maya signed for them even though she had no idea who they were from. She was still looking for a card when she heard Ayden's door open behind her, but she ignored him. She was curious who could have sent her flowers.

"Who are they from?" Ayden asked over her shoulder just as Maya found the card.

"Excuse me." She spun away from him, slid the small card from the envelope and read it. *Enjoyed your company last night. Have dinner with me, Ryan.*

A smile spread across Maya's lips.

"Well?" Ayden sounded annoyed when she still hadn't spoken. "Who are they from?"

"Ryan."

Ayden frowned. "Kincaid?"

Maya nodded and then swiveled around in her

chair to face the computer. She'd suspected Ryan was interested in her personally, but she'd never thought he'd act on it.

"What did the card say?"

Inflamed, Maya spun back around. First, Ayden wanted to ignore what had happened last night, and now he wanted to play twenty questions with her personal life? "What business is it of yours?"

His face turned red and Maya could see she'd angered him, but she didn't care. "The Kincaids are a client, an important one, so it darn well is my business."

"It has nothing to do with work," Maya replied hotly.

Ayden leaned down. Both his large hands bracketed her desk and made Maya feel caged in. "Did he ask you out?"

Her brow furrowed. "How would you know that?"

Ayden rose to his full height and glared at her. "Because it's what I would do. I saw the way he was looking at you."

"And just how was he looking at me?" Maya folded her arms across her chest. She dared Ayden to say more.

Ayden turned away from her for several moments, and when he faced her again, his features were schooled. "It's unseemly for you to accept dinner with a client."

"That's not fair!" Maya rose to her feet to confront him. She didn't appreciate Ayden implying that she would do anything that would harm Stewart Investments. She'd been a valuable employee for five years.

"You know I would never hurt you, I—I…" she stammered. "I mean hurt the company. And you *know* it."

Ayden colored. She'd hit her mark. "I apologize. I didn't mean to insinuate otherwise. So let me rephrase. It's not a good idea to mix business and pleasure."

"Is that a fact?" Her gaze met his and held. There was no mistaking she was referring to last night when he'd almost kissed her. Air bottled up in her lungs as she waited for a response.

Ayden had the grace to be embarrassed and looked away. "Do what you want!" He turned on his heel and slammed his door a moment later.

Maya told herself she didn't care how Ayden felt. She was being given an opportunity to go out with a good-looking, emotionally available man who was interested in her. Why not see where it led?

She glanced at Ayden's door. Because deep down, the man she wanted was closed off to her. Literally.

Ayden stared out his window for several moments before returning to his desk to concentrate on the figures and reports on his laptop, but it was useless. His brain was addled. Never before had he sat at his desk only to discover he'd wasted ten minutes thinking about a woman. And it wasn't just any woman. It was Maya. His Maya. He was imagining her going out with Ryan. Wondering if she'd kiss him. Let him touch her as he once had. He was jealous.

And he hated it.

He had no right to be.

He had no rights to Maya. But the thought of her with Kincaid stuck in his craw. He had seen the lust in the man's eyes when he'd looked at Maya. He had wanted to get to know her all right; he wanted to get to know her intimately! And worst of all, Maya didn't have a problem with it. He suspected she was doing it to give Ayden the finger for last night and today.

And she'd be within her rights.

He was falling back into old patterns. He'd acted as if he hadn't hauled her sensual, soft body against his hard one. Felt the pebbles of her nipples harden in response to their closeness. Heard her breath quicken as she anticipated a kiss between them. But he'd denied her. Denied them both. And now they were both miserable because they, or rather, *he* was trying to forget it happened.

It would have been easy if Maya was in her normal attire of navy skirt and button-down blouse. Except today, she'd chosen to wear a fuchsia-colored blouse that did wonders for her beautiful brown skin. He'd thought Maya returning to Stewart Investments was going to be easy. He had an active love life with plenty of women at his disposal. All he had to do was pick up the phone. There was no reason for him to feel like this; yet, he couldn't get his beautiful assistant out of his mind.

"Ayden?" Maya's voice rang through the intercom. "You have a call on line one."

He sighed. "I'm rather busy right now. Who is it?"

There was silence on the other end. "It's your sister, Fallon."

"I'll be with her in a moment." Ayden let go of the speaker button.

His *half sister*, Fallon. Four years younger than him, they shared the same DNA, but they had different mothers. He hated her witch of a mother, Nora Stewart, who was the cause of the downfall of his mother's marriage to Henry. The wily waitress had made sure she'd gotten pregnant and used it to lure his father away. Ayden had met Fallon a couple of times, but theirs certainly wasn't a normal brother-sister relationship. Why was she calling?

He had to know the answer. Ayden picked up the receiver. "Hello?"

"Ayden, it's so good to hear your voice. How are you?"

"I'm fine, Fallon. But I doubt this is a social call." The last time they'd seen each other had been six years ago when he'd expanded Stewart Investments and bought the building. Fallon had come to the grand opening. He'd been surprised by her appearance, as he was now by her call.

"Wow! I'd forgotten how you like to get to the point," Fallon said from the other end of the line.

"Yes, well, time is money."

"Of course. I was hoping if you had some free time, we might get together for lunch this week."

"I don't know." Ayden kept minimal contact with his half siblings. Although he couldn't blame them for their existence, Ayden still saw them as the chosen ones. The children that Henry deigned to acknowledge as his heirs while Ayden was left out in the cold to fend for himself.

"C'mon, Ayden. It's been several years. Aren't you the least bit curious about me? Dane?"

At times, he was. When he was lonely, Ayden wondered about his siblings and what they were doing with their lives. He knew Fallon ran Stewart Technologies, Henry's baby. Then there was his half brother.

Dane Stewart was an A-list actor in Hollywood. Ayden knew that Dane wanted no part of the Stewart family because he'd said so in several interviews. Ayden was certain there was a story behind Dane's estrangement and Fallon's absolute devotion. He'd even wondered what it would be like to have them as friends, but then he remembered that they'd had different lives. Ayden sighed heavily. "What is it that you want, Fallon?"

"Not over the phone," she whispered. "I need to speak with you privately. Can you meet me on Friday?"

Ayden was curious, so he agreed. "Yes, I'll have my assistant set it up."

"Thank you. I appreciate it. I'll see you then."

The line went dead, but Ayden was still holding the receiver. Exactly what did his sister want, and what did it have to do with him?

By Thursday, Maya was both giddy with excitement for her date with Ryan Kincaid this weekend and perturbed by Ayden's attitude the last couple of days. The only way she could describe his behavior

toward her was *chilly*. Ayden was not happy about
her spending time with Ryan. His interactions with
her were strictly business. Email this. Call this person. There was none of the warm camaraderie they
usually shared at the office.

He'd overheard Maya making plans with Ryan for
Saturday night after she'd called to thank him for the
beautiful arrangement. Since then, Ayden had been
acting like a sullen child. He barely spoke to her. He'd
been absent the last couple of days and was giving
her a wide berth. Maya supposed it was a good thing.
They'd gotten too close for comfort the other night.
If dating Ryan kept her from obsessing about Ayden
and wondering what might happen, it was for the best.

Callie agreed when she called Maya during lunch.
Her best friend was happy she was getting back
into the saddle and dating again. Maya knew Callie thought she was hopeless when it came to Ayden,
but she was over him. Or that's the white lie she told
Callie. If Ayden hadn't stopped that kiss, the heat between them would have consumed them. Maya refused to admit Ayden still held any power over her.
She would sweep what happened under the rug just
as he was doing.

After finishing lunch, she called her mother to
check in. As usual, Sophia was saying everything was
fine, but Maya knew better. True to her word, Raven
had emailed her copies of her mother's outstanding
medical bills, and since Raven had been authorized
on the account, Maya had been able to pay the clinic
directly without her mother being the wiser. She'd

also set up a payment plan for future bills. In addition, Raven had sent her mother's schedule, so Maya knew her chemo treatments were every three weeks, but hadn't yet mustered the courage to make one.

When she finally came back from her lunch break, she found Ayden sequestered in his office with the door shut. Maya continued working and filtering calls like she always did. When he was ready, he would come out and talk to her.

Eventually, her intercom buzzed. "Maya, can you make reservations tomorrow for a late lunch with my sister, Fallon, at two p.m."

The line went dead.

Ayden was lunching with his estranged sister, Fallon? How could he just drop a bomb like that and not expect her to ask questions?

One day, years ago, when Ayden had just won a lucrative client that would put Stewart Investments on the map, he'd confided in her about his past and how it had shaped him into the man he was today. Everyone was lauding him as the man with the Midas touch. All except one—his father.

Ayden had shared that deep down, he'd thought he might hear from Henry to say how proud he was of his accomplishments even though he'd done nothing to help him achieve them. Ayden told her that he knew he'd never get his father's love, but he'd wanted his acknowledgment. Despite all his successes, that day never came. And year after year, as Stewart Investments had grown, Maya had watched Ayden's heart grow harder where the Stewarts were concerned, which was why it was surprising he would agree to lunch with Fallon.

Maya worried about him and his well-being. She wanted to know if he'd be okay, but Ayden was shutting her out. Would he ever let anyone in?

Six

The next afternoon, Ayden walked purposefully through the restaurant. He'd made sure to dress for the occasion of meeting his estranged sister, choosing a custom-made suit, red tie and Italian loafers. He'd even gone to the barber to ensure his scalp was smooth as a baby's bottom and his five-o'clock shadow was well-groomed. If the princess of the Stewart family was deigning to meet with him, he had to look his best.

Fallon rose from her chair as he approached, and Ayden was reminded of just how beautiful his sister truly was. With her dark brown hair with honey blond streaks and her smooth café au lait skin, his sister was a knockout. A designer dress revealed her slender but curvy figure.

"Ayden, I'm so happy you agreed to meet me." His sister stared at him through hazel-gray eyes, the same as his. It was a family trait.

"Did I have a choice?" he asked, coming toward her and pushing her chair in as she sat down. If nothing else, his mother had raised a gentleman.

"I guess I didn't give you much of one," Fallon said after he sat across from her, "but given our relationship I wasn't sure you'd come."

"Curiosity brought me here," Ayden returned, placing his napkin in his lap. "I wondered why you would need anything from me, the black sheep of the family. The son our father can't be bothered to claim."

Sadness crossed her face and Fallon lowered her head. When she looked up again, tears were in the corners of her eyes. "I'm sorry Father has treated you this way, Ayden."

He shrugged. "What's it to you, anyway? You're his heir."

"And you're still my brother," she responded with a ferocity that shocked him.

"Now you want to claim me?" He smiled sardonically. "Why, Fallon? It's never been that important to you before."

"That's not fair, Ayden. I reached out to you when I went off to college, and you shot me down. You weren't interested in a little sister then."

"And I'm not interested in one now."

"Ouch." Fallon took that one on the chin, but bounced back, her eyes narrowing as she looked in his direction.

"Despite having grown up away from Father, you're just like him. You know how to hit below the belt."

Ayden sucked in a deep breath. He deserved that. He hadn't meant to be unkind, but it was a little late to play brother and sister. That time had come and gone. But, at the very least, she deserved to be treated with respect like any human being. "I'm sorry."

She raised a brow.

"I am," he insisted. "This is all a bit disconcerting."

Fallon gave him a half smile, and Ayden felt a kick in the gut because it warmed his cold heart to see it. "It is for me, as well. It wasn't easy calling you for help, but I did."

"Help?"

"I'm in trouble, Ayden."

Ayden sat upright in his seat, training his gaze on her beautiful facial bones. "What kind of trouble? What can I do to help?"

"Careful, Ayden," Fallon said with humor to her tone. "You almost sounded like a big brother there."

His eyes narrowed. "What do you need, Fallon?"

"I don't know if you knew, but I'm CFO of Stewart Technologies. Have been a few years now."

"I'd heard."

"Have you also heard that the company isn't doing well? We've been in trouble for several quarters now. I've been doing my best to contain the damage, but bad investments and poor project planning have crippled the company. I've tried my best to turn it around, but there's little hope of saving it now."

Ayden frowned. He didn't like the direction this conversation was heading, but he was here now and he had no choice but to listen. It would be rude of him to get up and walk away, even though that's exactly what he wanted to do.

"For years, I tried to get Father to listen to me, but he's stubborn and pigheaded. Determined to do things his way, and now we're in a bind. We need a bailout."

And there it was, Ayden thought. The catch that had brought Fallon to contact him out of the blue. She needed money. "And what is it you expect me to do?"

"Ayden." Fallon reached across the table, which seemed as wide as an ocean, and took his hand. "I've heard great things about you. Everyone's calling you the miracle worker. If anyone can help turn this around it's you. And…" She paused as if searching for her words. "With some of your financial backing we could save the company."

Ayden stared at Fallon in disbelief. He glanced around the room to see if anyone had heard, because he wasn't sure he'd heard right. Fallon, Nora's daughter with Henry, was asking him, the son Henry had cast aside, to save *her* father's company. Surely, she had lost her mind. "And why would I want to do a thing like that?"

"Because it's our family business."

"No, Fallon. It's *your* family business. Stewart Investments is *my* business."

"But…"

"There's no buts. Henry chose to divorce my mother and walk away from us, and that's fine. That's his choice, but when he did, he washed his hands of me and subsequently any allegiance I had to this—" he made air quotes with his hands "—family."

"Ayden, I know you're upset with Father."

"Upset?" His voice rose and when it did, several patrons looked in his direction. "*Upset* is acting as if we had a minor disagreement, Fallon. I'm not upset. I *hate* him. I hate him for how he treated me, but most of all for how he treated my mother. He left her with nothing, even though she helped him start that damn company."

Tears sprang to her beautiful eyes—so like his own. "Wh-what? I thought—but my mother said..."

"Your mother lied, Fallon. Lillian Stewart was the woman behind the man, working two jobs to get Henry through college so he could work on his degree, helping build the capital necessary to open Stewart Technologies. And when he became successful, he kicked her to the curb for a younger model and cheated her out of her rightful share of the company. So Fallon, there's not a snowball's chance in hell I would ever help that man or his company and, unfortunately, that affects you." Ayden rose to his feet.

"Ayden," Fallon rushed out of her seat and placed a firm hand on his arm, stopping him before he'd taken two steps past her. "Please don't leave this way. I had no idea about what happened to you and your mother. I wasn't even born. Surely, you can't blame me?"

"I know that, Fallon, and I don't blame you. Henry's mistakes are his and his alone. I came here today out of respect for you even when I didn't have to. I heard you out, but there's nothing left to say." He glanced down at her hand on his sleeve, but she held on firmer.

Her eyes implored his and he saw the fear in them. "I need your help."

"I'm sorry, but the answer is no. Let the company crash and burn because, quite frankly, that's exactly what Henry so richly deserves." Ayden wrenched his arm away and spun on his heel. His heart was thudding loudly in his chest and his pulse was racing. He quickly threaded his way through the tables until he made it to the door. Once he was outside, he leaned against the building's facade and inhaled deeply.

Rage was coursing through his veins. Not at Fallon, but at Henry for ruining the company his mother helped build. Ayden wanted to punch something, *someone*, but instead he walked. And walked. He would walk back to the office so he could cool off and let calmer heads prevail.

Maya glanced down at her watch. It was well after five o'clock and the office was starting to clear out, but Maya couldn't leave. She hadn't heard from Ayden all afternoon and she was worried. He hadn't returned from his lunch with his half sister. Maya was dying to know how it went and if he was okay, but he hadn't so much as called to check in for messages.

It was nearly six when she finally gave up and began packing up her belongings. She was turning off the lights when she saw Ayden walking toward her from the reception area. Instead of his usual long and confident stride, his shoulders were hunched over.

As he drew closer, Maya could see anguish etched across his face.

"Ayden?"

He glanced up, but looked straight through her and walked into his office. Maya was rooted to the spot as conflicting emotions tore through her. Should she go after him? He appeared so forlorn. Lost even, if she had to put a name on it. Or she should she go home and let him figure it out alone? They'd agreed to have a purely business relationship. Getting involved would complicate things.

But she couldn't leave him like that, could she?

Making a split decision, Maya threw down her things and headed for his door. She was surprised to find it ajar. He was sitting on the couch with his head hung low, a bottle of liquor on the table in front of him. A glass of dark liquid was in his hands. Maya suspected it was the aged cognac he kept on hand for celebrating a victory or sweet deal. But today was different. He was drowning his sorrows, whatever they may be.

She walked toward him quietly. He didn't say a word when she sat beside him. Instead, he continued drinking. When he'd finished the first glass, he poured himself another. They sat in silence for an eternity before Maya spoke. She was dying to know what happened. "Ayden?"

"Hmm...?"

"Are you okay?"

"No." He took another sip of his drink.

Ayden wasn't talkative by nature, but when he was

in this mood, he would be even less forthcoming. "Did something happen at your lunch with Fallon?"

He turned to glare at her. The full force of his piercing hazel stare rested solely on her, and Maya squirmed in her seat at the intensity. "What do you think?"

Maya swallowed. She had to push and break through the barrier Ayden had erected to protect himself. She understood because she'd done the same thing herself. "What happened?"

"I don't want to talk about it."

"Perhaps if you didn't hold it inside, you might feel better," Maya offered.

"Feel?" Ayden huffed. "I don't want to feel anything."

Maya blinked several times, but tried again. "Ayden…" She touched his arm and he shrank away from her. Jumping to his feet, he made for the window on the far side of the room.

"Don't touch me, Maya. Not right now. You should go home." He turned away from her to face the window.

"I can't go home and leave you like this. You're hurting and I want to help."

He spun to face her. "You can't help me, Maya. No one can. Unless you can erase the last thirty years and make my father love me, want me—" he beat his chest with his fist "—acknowledge me as his son. His firstborn. The rightful heir to Stewart Technologies."

"Oh, Ayden."

"Don't!" He pointed his finger at her, tumbler still

in hand. "Don't you dare feel sorry for me! I won't have it."

"Okay, okay." Maya held up her hands in surrender as she walked toward him. She took the glass out of his hand and placed it on a nearby table. He watched her with keen eyes, his chest rising and falling. "You don't have my pity. But I'm here for you, Ayden."

Heavy awareness surged through her as she locked gazes with him. Maya swallowed, but her mouth felt dry and parched. She inched forward until they were standing a breath away from each other. Something fundamental changed as they stared at each other, something that electrified the airspace. Maya was afraid to speak, afraid to break the interlude.

Maya touched his arm and when she glanced up, Ayden's gaze had turned from tortured to hot and burning. She should move away and get out of the office fast, but she couldn't seem to stop herself. There was so much tension inside him. Tension she wanted to help relieve. As if pulled by some imperceptible thread, her body moved closer to his. Maya felt the heat of him in her lower half as their bodies brushed once, twice. Then Ayden's hand flew to the small of her back and pressed her forward, clamping her tight against him.

Air whooshed out of Maya's lungs, but that didn't stop her from tipping her head upward and peeking up at him from beneath her lashes. She shouldn't have done that because with that movement, she swayed into his space. Ayden leaned forward until they were chest to chest, and then he kissed her. Their lips touched slowly, hesitantly at first, as if they were both unsure of whether they should continue, but then Ayden shifted, and Maya felt the strain of his erection against her middle and the kiss erupted.

Her mouth opened under his and he swept her into his embrace, kissing her deeply. Before she knew it, Maya's back was hitting the window, but she scarcely noticed because she was coming alive under Ayden's skillful mouth. His hands were threading through her hair and his mouth was devouring hers. Hunger coursed through her, and she thrust her hips involuntarily against his as an ache began to claim her lower region.

Ayden grasped her hips and tightened his arms around her, tipping her head to just the right angle so he could stroke his tongue with hers. Over and over again, he stroked her, deeper, harder and faster until he had Maya moaning in pleasure. She cupped the back of his neck and his hands roamed over her. When he found her breasts, he molded and kneaded them with his palm. He was luring her into a dark pit of need and Maya was drowning. She felt his hands snake under her dress, felt him touch her thigh.

Please, oh God, she wanted him to touch her there. She tilted her hips in silent invitation, begging him to do whatever he desired.

And just as his hands began inching to the damp place between her thighs, a knock sounded on the door. "Housekeeping."

Maya jumped back as if a bucket of cold water had been thrown on them. She glanced at the door and then back at Ayden. His face was a storm of desire and Maya licked her lips.

"Do that again and I'll have you on the desk and to hell who sees us."

Maya blushed and, without saying a word, rushed for the door, swung it open and fled from the room. She ran past the stunned cleaner standing just outside the door, grabbed her purse and made for the elevator. She didn't dare look behind her because she couldn't look at Ayden. Not after what had just happened between them. If that cleaner hadn't knocked on the door when she had, who knew what would have happened.

Maya knew exactly what would have happened.

She would have allowed Ayden to make love to her again. And then where would she be? Back at square one.

Ayden slammed his fists down on his desk. He hadn't meant for that to happen, but Maya had gotten too close to the sun. And if she wasn't careful, she would get burned. That was exactly how he felt right now. Like scorched earth. Seeing Fallon had resurrected his demons. Ayden didn't talk about his family *ever* except the one time with Maya. She was the only person who knew he'd been abandoned by the great technical genius Henry Stewart.

But it wasn't exactly true. Ayden could remember a time when he was younger, before the divorce, when his father had been in his life. He'd been about five years old. He recalled his parents together, happy, but then Nora had come into the picture. Ayden had vague recollections of his mother and Henry arguing. His mother accusing Henry of being unfaithful. Ayden remembered finding Lillian crying in her bedroom because his father had asked her to leave.

Leave *her* house. And she had. She hadn't fought for what was hers—what was due her after she'd helped him build the company. Instead, she'd allowed that evil witch Nora to play lady of the manor in their home while he and his mother had been kicked out. Ayden blamed Henry for all the hardships they'd endured, the mental and physical abuse at Jack's hands. So there was no way in hell he would bail that man out of trouble. Let the company crumble. It was what Henry had coming. He was sorry Fallon was caught in the crossfire, but she was a grown woman and it was her decision to run the company. She would have to figure her own way out.

But Maya. Maya was another story. She'd only been trying to help, to lend a sympathetic ear, and he'd taken advantage of her. *You're weak.* The nasty voice of his conscience called him out. He'd let himself indulge in her when he'd given her his word that he would behave. If he couldn't keep the promises he'd made, he was no better than his louse of a father Henry, who hadn't kept his marital vows.

Ayden closed his eyes, but it did little to erase the imprint of Maya from his senses. He could still smell her sweet scent in the air. How in the world was he going to be able to forget how she tasted and go back to a professional relationship?

Seven

The next morning, Maya awoke feeling more exhausted than she'd been before going to bed. When she'd arrived home, she'd paced, unable to sleep because she couldn't get the kiss with Ayden off her mind. So she'd pretty much clock-watched the entire night, and time had seemed to stagnate.

Throwing back the covers, Maya showered and threw on her gear to go for a run. When she was in a mood like this, running was the best cure. She waved at her building's security guard and started for a nearby park about half a mile away. Maybe she could lose herself on the trail and feel invigorated afterward.

An hour later, Maya felt no better. In fact, she felt terribly silly for making a mountain out of a molehill. It was just a kiss. But was it?

Ayden wasn't just *any* man. He was the man of her dreams. The man whose face she had been unable to forget for five long years. And now, during her run, he was all Maya could think of. The kiss had stirred up past feelings Maya thought she'd resolved. It had been earth-shatteringly passionate. It had rocked Maya to the core and made her wonder whether she could continue working for Ayden.

Maya realized that they'd never really resolved what happened five years ago. Instead, they'd acted like it was a one-time thing because she'd been upset over Thomas. She'd thought it had been pity, but now she realized that was a lie. If they'd both been bold enough, they'd admit there was something *there*. An attraction simmering just below the surface. Under the right circumstances and conditions, they combusted.

How else could she explain why Ayden had kissed her last night and she'd kissed him back? She'd been a willing and active participant in that kiss. Her heart thundered with excitement at how passionate Ayden had been. She'd felt the full force of that unleashed energy and doubted they would have stopped if not for the well-timed knock on the door.

Knowing that she felt this way, there was no way she could go out for dinner tonight with Ryan. Not when she had these swirling emotions surrounding Ayden on her mind. Once she made it to Starbucks for a coffee, Maya went to a quiet corner to make her call.

Ryan answered after several rings. "Maya, good morning."

"Good morning, Ryan. How are you?"

"I'm excited for our date this evening."

"Listen, about that—"

"Don't tell me you're canceling?" Ryan interrupted.

"I don't think it's a good idea that we go out," Maya said. "I really can't handle anything other than friendship right now. I have a lot going on in my life."

"Friendship sounds like a great start. Let's scratch dinner. How about attending a polo match?"

"Polo?" Maya had never been to a match and understood nothing of the game.

"Yes, polo. You can put on your Sunday best, well, in this case, your Saturday best, and meet me at the Austin Polo Club."

"I don't know...." Maya recalled that Ayden loved the sport. He used to talk about how he and Luke had played it during undergrad. Was he still playing for this club? But what if he were? Did it really matter? With all the people attending, it was highly doubtful he would even notice her.

"Do you have other plans?"

"No, but..."

"I'll see you at two then." Seconds later, the call ended and Maya was staring down at her phone. Ryan had hung up without giving her a chance to change her mind. Very sneaky of him. But she didn't have any plans, and if Ryan was okay that all she had to offer was friendship, then why not? She hadn't been out with anyone other than Ayden since she'd returned to Austin. It would be nice to have some male companionship, even if was a non-date. And who knows? Polo could be fun.

* * *

Ayden needed physical exertion to help clear his mind and give him some perspective on why he kept screwing up royally with Maya. He'd already gone to the gym this morning for two hours and was happy he had a polo match scheduled for even more punishment.

All morning as he'd hit the treadmill, weights, even the boxing ring, his mind kept wandering to Maya. And how he'd been greedy for her last night. He'd wanted to feel her skin against his. Had wanted to kiss her, touch her, and if that knock hadn't interrupted them, he would have taken her everywhere—up against the window, the desk, the floor, the couch in his office. He wouldn't have cared, because she'd spiked a need in him he couldn't recall feeling in… well….in five years. When that very same need had rocked him to his core and caused him to push her away.

Ayden hadn't understood it then and darn sure didn't understand it now. Maya was his assistant, his friend, yet she was the only woman who fired up a lust in him that was so profound he lost all thought or reason. She made him impulsive rather than cool and in control like he usually was in sexual encounters.

He had to get himself back on track, and today's match at the Austin Polo Club would help. After the gym, he'd gone home to shower and get ready for the game. He'd donned his usual ensemble of well-worn riding boots that fit just below the knees, white riding breeches and a black polo shirt with the number 3 for his position in the polo club. He liked being the attacker. And today, there was a tournament against a club out of San Antonio and he was ready for battle.

When he arrived at the club, he hopped out of his Bentley, gave his keys to one of the many valets and grabbed his gloves, kneepads and helmet with chin strap. He was looking forward to running his polo pony, a beautiful Thoroughbred he'd purchased some years back. He could thank Luke for introducing him to the sport in New England, because it had stuck. Ayden had found the polo club and been a member ever since. He typically tried to play twice a month to ensure he and his pony were one on the field, which in this case was the size of six soccer fields.

When he arrived at the stables, which housed two hundred Thoroughbreds, his team was already getting ready for the tournament. Ayden wasted no time saddling up his pony, and braiding and wrapping its tail. Once he was ready, he swung his leg around and into the stirrups. A club hand was on board to help, handing him his helmet and mallet.

"You ready to give those San Antonio boys a whooping and send them home?" Eddie, a venture capitalist and one of his team members, asked when he was mounted.

"Heck, yeah!" Ayden responded.

The first chukka went supremely well with Austin making the first goal. Ayden was really getting into the game. And when the umpire threw the ball between the two teams on the second chukka, Ayden took off after it with a fury, challenging the opposing San Antonio team member by riding him off. It worked. It moved his opponent away from the ball and out of the play so his teammate could score a goal.

"Good job!" Mateo, another of his team members, yelled as they began leading their ponies back to the equestrian facility for a break.

"Thanks, I was in the..." Ayden's sentence was cut short when he spied Maya and Ryan stepping out on the field to stomp the divots. What was she doing here? And with Ryan of all people?

Ayden was furious. Uncaring of who was watching, he began riding his pony across the field in Maya's direction.

"Having fun?" Ryan asked as he led Maya onto the green so they could stomp the grass.

"Oh, yes," Maya said, smiling from ear to ear. "Thanks for suggesting this." She hadn't the foggiest notion what to wear to a polo match. The only other time she'd seen one was when she'd watched Julia Roberts in *Pretty Woman*.

Did she need a big hat? She hadn't brought one with her. After rummaging through the closet, Maya had found a lace-embroidered off-shoulder white jumpsuit with wide leg pants. She'd matched it with some chunky wedges and large hoop earrings. She thought she looked pretty good. And when she'd met Ryan he'd agreed by giving her an appreciative whistle. He looked equally casual in a pair of Dockers, a polo shirt and a blazer.

"My pleasure." Ryan's mouth curved into a grin. "To be honest," he said, stomping the green with his foot, "I'd be happy with any time I got to spend with you."

Maya glanced up at him and there was no mistaking the interest in his gaze. Ryan wanted more than friendship, but that's all she had to give him. Her relationship with Ayden was too complicated for her to bring someone else into the picture, no matter how great he might be.

She wanted to say more, but then she heard hooves, and when she glanced up, she saw Ayden barreling down on them. Ryan grasped her by the waist and pushed her behind him as Ayden barely stopped his horse in enough time in front of them. Maya sucked in a deep breath at the near miss and noticed the lethal glint in Ayden's hazel eyes.

"Ayden, in God's name, man, you could have killed us," Ryan lashed out.

"Hardly," Ayden said, hurtling himself over the pony and pulling the animal forward by the reins. "I take care of what's mine."

The possessive look he gave Maya caused her stomach to knot up and her throat to suddenly become very dry. Was he talking about her? Because she wasn't his. She never had been and doubted she ever would be. He didn't do commitments. She'd always known that.

"What are you doing here?" Ayden inquired. There was an edge to his voice that Maya didn't understand.

"You invited me, remember?" Ryan replied. "At the restaurant."

"Ah yes." Ayden nodded and his voice became mellower. "I forgot. Though I had no idea you were bringing Maya." He glanced in her direction again, his gaze traveling from the wedges on her feet to the one-piece jumpsuit showing off her bare shoulders.

Maya finally found her voice even though her throat felt parched. "It was a last-minute thing, but I'm glad I came."

"Is that so?" Ayden's brow furrowed.

The level of tension between them ratcheted up and Maya's nerves were stretched tight. "Yes, that's right." She didn't appreciate his tone. He was acting as if she'd done something untoward when she'd only accepted a simple invitation to a polo match. *During the day.* It wasn't as if they were on a date. But weren't they? Even though Ryan had suggested it under the guise of "just friends," she knew he wanted more. But he also hadn't given her the chance to say no, having hung up before she could respond.

"Glad you're enjoying your date," Ayden said. "Be sure to watch me on the field." He jumped onto the back of the horse with ease and, after a swift kick, they were gone.

Ryan turned and eyed her. "What the hell was that about?"

Maya shrugged as if she didn't have a clue, but

she knew. Ayden was jealous. Jealous over the fact that she was here with Ryan on what he thought was a romantic date when they were just friends. But why not let Ayden stew on it? He had no claims on her, and it would be good for Ayden Stewart to eat a little humble pie.

Ayden was angry. He didn't like how cozy Maya and Ryan were. Didn't like the level of intimacy he'd witnessed between them. Not one bit. He'd arrived back at the equestrian facility to cool the pony down and have a refreshment.

Although he didn't want a relationship with Maya, he didn't want Ryan to have her, either. Which was totally unfair. Maya deserved someone better, who would treat her well, marry her and father a gaggle of babies. It's what she'd always wanted and thought she might have with the knucklehead who'd married her sister. Instead, she was in limbo with Ayden because he kept giving her mixed messages. They had a professional relationship one day. And the next, he was kissing her senseless and muddying the waters. Ayden couldn't make sense of it. He knew his jealousy was irrational, but he seemed powerless to control it.

"Are you going to keep daydreaming, Stewart, or are you ready to win this thing?" Eddie said from above him.

Ayden glanced up and found his team was already back in the saddle. "Yeah, I'm ready. I'm ready to pummel them." He hopped back onto his pony and they headed onto the field. He was going to win this thing. He had an audience and wanted to show Maya how skilled he was at polo. Of course, there were other skills he'd rather show her, which included the two of them on a bed or whatever surface was available.

He blinked. *Get your head out of the clouds, Stewart*, he reminded himself as the umpire threw the ball. Ayden took off down the field.

Unfortunately, the San Antonio team must have regrouped during halftime because they came back stronger than ever and won the third and fourth chukka, forcing a draw. Now they had to play another chukka, and the first team to score would win. Ayden wasn't playing his best and he knew it. Every time he got a chance, he was looking across the field, trying to find Maya, wondering what she was doing with Ryan. It was driving him crazy.

All four team members had gathered for a pep talk. "Come on, guys," Mateo commanded. "We've got to win this, otherwise we don't get to the Centennial Cup. So let's do this."

"Let's do it!" they all yelled.

Fired up, Ayden went all in. As soon as the ball was in the air, he rode toward his man. Ayden bumped the other player with his shoulder while simultaneously attempting another maneuver to hook his mallet when his opponent hit the ball. But their mallets got tangled together and both ponies began to get agitated. Before he knew it, Ayden was hurtling through the air and hit the ground with a loud thump.

* * *

Ayden had a splitting headache. Furtively he glanced around the room and that's when he realized he was at the hospital. The last thing he remembered was getting tangled up with the opposing player at the polo match and flying through the air. How long had he been out? He couldn't remember, he just knew he hated hospitals. That was where his mom had died. He tried to move, but felt immobile. Glancing down, Ayden saw a compression wrap around his ankle.

He couldn't afford any broken limbs. He led an active life and had a full workload. He wiggled his ankle. Thankfully, he could move it, but it was definitely swollen. He pressed the buzzer for a nurse. Several minutes later, one walked in. Dressed in blue scrubs and a white jacket, the young brunette came toward him to take his vitals.

"Ah, you've awoken from your slumber," she said.

"How long was I out?"

"For a while. You have a mild concussion, a contusion on your left eye and a sprained ankle, but otherwise, you'll be fine."

"Is that all?" he asked snarkily. "When can I get out of here?" He used the remote to lift the bed upward into a sitting position. He hated feeling helpless.

"Not tonight," the nurse replied. "We're keeping you overnight for observation, but I'm sure the doctor will release you tomorrow into the care of a loved one."

The care of a loved one. He didn't have anyone here because Luke was across the ocean. His mother had been the only family he'd ever had. And as far as Fallon or Dane, he doubted either of them would come to his aid. The only person he could think of, the only person he would want taking care of him, was Maya. Maya cared for him and would be willing to help. And what better way to ensure she stayed away from Ryan than keeping her close by his side.

Oh, yes, Maya was the right person for the job.

Eight

Maya anxiously paced the hospital waiting room. How long was it going to take for them to tell her something? She'd been waiting for hours to hear about Ayden's condition and no one would tell her anything because she wasn't family. Ryan had stayed with her, but eventually she'd told him to go home. There was nothing he could do and she wasn't leaving until she could see for herself that Ayden was okay. Ryan had understood and advised her to sort through her feelings for Ayden.

When she thought about the accident, her heart turned over in her chest. She'd gasped in horror when Ayden had fallen from the horse. Immediately, she'd run to him, uncaring of how it might look to Ryan or anyone else. She'd just known she had to get to

Ayden. He'd been lying motionless on the green and was unresponsive until the ambulance had arrived. He'd opened his eyes briefly on the ride to the hospital, and she hadn't seen those beautiful hazel-gray eyes since.

Once they'd arrived, she'd been treated like a second-class citizen and sent to the waiting room because she wasn't family. No one would talk to her until finally she'd pleaded for any word. They'd told her he was stable, but nothing more.

"Ms. Richardson?" a female voice called out from behind her.

Maya spun around and rushed toward the nurse. "Is there any news on Mr. Stewart?"

"Yes, ma'am. He's awake and asking for you."

Thank God! Maya closed her eyes and said a silent prayer. "Take me to him."

"Follow me."

The nurse led her into a private room. Ayden was sitting on the bed, fully awake with his ankle wrapped. He had one black eye, and a bandage was wrapped over the other side of his head, covering his left eye. Maya rushed toward him and, without thinking, flung herself into his arms. He clutched her to his hard chest.

"It's okay." Ayden patted her back as if he were comforting a small child. "I'm all right, Maya. I have a concussion and a sprained ankle, but other than that, I'm fine."

Inhaling, Maya counted to three and slowly rose to her feet. She'd overreacted and shown her true feelings. "I'm so relieved." Then she reached across the distance and swatted his arm. "Don't ever scare me like that again."

Ayden gave her a sideways grin. "Hey, I'm sorry. Didn't mean to give you a scare. Or sprain any ligaments." He nodded downward toward his ankle.

"Serves you right for those moves you pulled," Maya replied. "Ryan told me not many people try both those moves together."

"I had to do something. We were going to lose."

"And now look at you. You're going to have to take it easy. Maybe use the time for a much-needed vacation."

"I don't vacation," Ayden responded. "I have a business to run. I just need someone to help me while I'm…" He searched for the right word. "Incapacitated."

"Good luck. You're not an easy man to deal with."

"I don't need luck. I just need you."

"Me?" She hadn't been prepared for such a blunt, matter-of-fact statement.

"I need a nursemaid who can take care of me and help me navigate the next week, and I can't think of anyone more qualified than you."

"A-Ayden, that's crazy. I'm no nursemaid. I'm just your assistant."

"True, but you know me. You know what I like and dislike better than any other person," he replied. "You can do this, Maya. Unless there's a reason you can't?"

"What are you talking about?"

"I'm talking about Ryan Kincaid. You were with him at the polo match. In that outfit." He motioned toward her jumpsuit, which showed off her figure and a small swell of cleavage. "I know he's interested in you. Is the feeling mutual? Is that why you can't do me this favor?"

So he was jealous of Ryan. She knew it! But what would make Ayden think she could possibly get involved with another man after the kiss they'd shared last night? Ryan was just a friend, but Ayden didn't know that. It served him right that he was jealous. Over the years, she'd listened to him expound on plenty of other women.

Ayden's behavior didn't make any sense. He'd had a chance with her five years ago. But Ayden hadn't wanted her then. So what had changed?

Why now?

"Well?" Ayden was looking at Maya and waiting for an answer.

"I don't have to justify my actions to you or anyone, Ayden."

He glared at her and she could see he wanted to say more. She'd read between the lines with him long enough to know he was biting his tongue. He contemplated her for several long moments, his gaze scraping her from head to toe. It was a standoff that Maya intended to win.

"You're correct," he said, his voice softening. "I have no right to interfere in your personal life. I was out of line. But I am asking you for your help. You know me—and my needs and wants—better than anyone else. I want you."

Those words sank her. Her belly somersaulted in

the air and did a triple axel like an ice skater, but she mustn't let it. She couldn't do this. There was no way that in spending time with Ayden, day in and day out, her true feelings for him wouldn't be exposed. "I'm sorry. I can't." Maya turned away. She couldn't look at him because doing so was playing tricks with her emotions.

"Maya, please," Ayden implored from the bed. "I'll double your salary. Whatever it takes. I *need* you."

Maya reminded herself to stay strong, but when she swirled around to face him, the pleading look in his eyes stopped her cold. There was no way she could deny this man anything even though it wasn't in her best interests. "Okay. Okay, I'll do it."

A large grin spread over his gorgeous face despite the bandage across his eye. "I knew you wouldn't let me down," he said smugly. "You should probably get back to the rental and pack up your things. I'll have a driver bring your belongings to my mansion."

"Your house?" she squeaked.

"Of course. You can't possibly take care of me from your apartment. You'll need to move in, temporarily that is, until I get on my feet."

"I can't move in with you, Ayden."

"Why not?"

Because I'm in love with you. Because we kissed last night and almost had sex in your office the night before. Maya's face grew hot with a blush and she responded, "It's just not a good idea."

"Rubbish. It makes the most sense for you to be

close by. So run along and collect your things and I'll have my driver meet you in a couple of hours."

"You can't just run roughshod over me, Ayden."

"I'm not trying to, but you must see how ridiculous it sounds for you to be my nursemaid from your apartment."

When he put it like that, it made Maya appear silly for suggesting such a thing. "Fine. Fine," she agreed begrudgingly.

"Good. I'm glad that's settled. Make yourself comfortable at my place. Feel free to choose any room you like. And then be back here tomorrow morning because that's when they're releasing me."

"Is there anything else, boss?" Because that was exactly the tone he'd used with her. Not the sexy way he said her name last night in the heat of passion.

"I'm sorry. I didn't mean to sound so formal, Maya. I really appreciate you doing this for me."

She nodded and before she could put a foot in her mouth again, Maya left the room. She needed some air anyway. Ayden had used her affection for him to lure her into his home. Now they would be sharing close quarters. How on earth was she supposed to keep her cool?

It didn't take long for Maya to pack up her meager belongings. And as promised, the driver called her when he arrived at the apartment building. He and the bellhop helped put all her suitcases into the limousine. Maya got in and leaned back against the buttery soft leather interior. It wasn't her first trip in a limousine.

She'd accompanied Ayden on many occasions when they'd worked together. But it was quite different to be treated to this kind of luxury on her own.

Leaning back, she closed her eyes. Maya couldn't believe she was doing this. Not only had she accepted her old executive assistant position, but somehow she'd allowed Ayden to convince her to serve as his nursemaid *and* move into his home? It was insanity. But it had been impossible to deny him, especially after he'd said he needed her. *Wanted* her.

Of course, she knew he hadn't meant it like he had last night. That had been a moment in time, when he'd been in pain and reached for the nearest person to comfort him. She'd been convenient. She was a woman and he was a man. A man used to getting sex. Ayden had wanted to escape his past and she'd been willing. Like any red-blooded man, he'd accepted what she was offering.

She searched her purse for her phone. She'd called Callie after Ayden's accident and been beside herself. Callie had calmed her down, but would still be worried.

"Maya." Callie picked up on the first ring. "How is Ayden?"

"He's okay. He has a concussion and a sprained ankle, but he's okay."

"Thank God! I had no idea polo matches could be so dangerous."

"From what Ryan told me, they usually aren't, but Ayden was playing aggressively and making bold moves."

"Sounds like Ayden was jealous seeing you with another man. Do you think he was showboating to garner your attention?"

Maya was silent for a moment as she drank more of her champagne. "It's doubtful. He just wasn't exactly happy that I was with a client."

"A client? You mean another man?"

"I dunno," she fibbed. Because she'd thought the same thing. And she just had to spit out why she'd called. "Anyway, you should know I've agreed to move in and help Ayden around the house and at work until he's back on his feet."

"Sweet baby Jesus!" Callie retorted. "Out of the frying pan and into the fire. Don't you ever learn, girlfriend? What on earth possessed you to agree to such a thing?"

"He needs me. Please, be supportive, Callie. I need you to understand."

"Oh, Lord, Maya. I'm just scared that you're going to get hurt."

"I'll be okay. I can handle this." Or at least she hoped so, because if not, Callie was right. Ayden had the power to truly devastate her, so much so that she might never recover.

Nine

"Comfortable?" Maya asked once she'd settled Ayden in his master bedroom, fluffing his pillows and tucking the covers around him. She'd arrived late that morning to pick him up from the hospital. She'd come prepared with a change of clothes for him consisting of a tracksuit.

He smiled. He was more than comfortable. He was on cloud nine because Maya was here with him. Truth be told, when he'd made the outrageous suggestion, he'd expected her to turn him down flat. She'd put up some resistance, but in the end, he'd persevered and convinced her to move in with him. And with her tending to his needs day and night, there was no way she would have time to see Ryan Kincaid.

Was he really that jealous of his client?

Yes.

He hadn't liked seeing Maya spending time or having fun with another man. Her smile was reserved for only him.

"Yes, I'm comfortable, Maya. Thank you," he finally answered.

She'd been busy since last night. She'd placed crutches nearby to help him get around on his own. He could see her touches in the room, too. There were freshly cut flowers on the nightstand. His favorite spy books had been neatly stacked beside them along with a bottle of water and some pain pills. She'd filled his prescription. She'd literally thought of everything.

It was why he'd wanted her here with him.

Or at least it was one of the reasons. If he was honest with himself, it went deeper, beyond a friend caring for another friend, but he couldn't think like that. She was just doing him a favor.

"Is there anything you'd like?" Maya inquired.

You, Ayden thought as he peered at her through thick lashes. Today, she was dressed in slim-fitting jeans that showed off her sweet behind along with a long-sleeved sweater that had cutout shoulders. She was hardly wearing any makeup other than some mascara and some type of gloss that made her lips shine. He wanted to lean over, grab her by the waist and kiss it off. Although she might appear plain to some, Ayden thought she'd never looked lovelier. Lord, he was in a world of trouble.

"I'd like to go through any outstanding proposals

including the Kincaids' to make sure they don't need tweaking before you send them out."

"You want to work?" Maya inquired with a frown. "For Christ's sake, you just got out of the hospital and are recovering from a concussion. Not to mention it's a Sunday, Ayden. I don't work on the weekends. So if you want this arrangement—" she pointed between the two of them "—to work, then you're going to have to remember those parameters."

"All right, what would you suggest we do? I can think of a few." Even with a bum leg, he had a few ideas, but they were certainly not PG-13.

"How about a movie? Or we could marathon a television show on Netflix."

"I don't watch TV."

Maya rose from her seat. "That's too bad because I'm going to find an activity for us that doesn't require the use of a bed."

He bowled over with laughter as he watched her scoot out of the room.

Maya was happy for some breathing room. She knew what other ideas he had because her mind immediately went to imagining the two of them naked, sprawled out over his sumptuous covers, kissing and making wild, passionate love. She'd felt her cheeks grow warm. Had Ayden sensed where her mind had wandered?

Probably not.

She was just a means to end, taking care of his immediate needs while making sure the office ran smoothly in his absence. Would he ever see her as more? Did she want him to?

Her mind was swirling as she set about locating the butler. She had to find some activity to keep the two of them busy on her day off. Because she was sure, come tomorrow, Ayden would be ready to get back to work, sprained ankle or not.

She found the butler downstairs in the kitchen talking to the chef about dinner. "Good afternoon, Ms. Richardson. Is there anything I can help you with?" he asked.

"First, you can call me, Maya." When he began to interrupt her, she held up her hand. "I'm going to be staying here while your boss recovers, so please call me by my first name."

"Very well, Maya. And second?"

"Do you have cable, internet, Netflix, anything to amuse us?"

A half hour later, Maya was armed and ready to entertain. The butler had secured a television and DVR on wheels and brought it into Ayden's master suite. Ayden had always told her he much preferred reading a good book or engaging in extracurricular activities with the opposite sex to watching mindless television. The butler had also found several board games like chess and dominoes and Taboo to keep their minds occupied until dinner. Meanwhile, she'd thrown some popcorn she'd found in the pantry into the microwave.

"What's all this?" Ayden asked when they brought in all the goodies.

"Your education on being an everyday joe," Maya said with a smile. "We're going to watch movies, eat popcorn and veg out all day."

"Really?"

"That's right, and you're going to love it."

And they did. While munching on popcorn, Maya joined Ayden on his bed—*above the covers*—and made him watch *Pretty Woman*. And instead of going downstairs to a formal dinner in his dining salon, dinner was served to them on television trays. Afterward, they ended up playing a game of chess. Ayden absolutely killed her.

"No fair," Maya said when the game was over. "You're a master at this. When did you learn how to play?"

Ayden shrugged. "I learned chess at boarding school. We didn't have much else to do. Thanks to my stepfather, I knew how to hustle those rich kids out of their money. For them, it wasn't a hardship, but for me it ensured I had spending money because my stepfather didn't allow Mom to send me any money at school. He was just glad to be rid of me."

"What happened during school breaks?"

"I usually begged to go to friends' houses. Sometimes it worked. Sometimes Jack tolerated me coming home, but he made sure I knew that I was only there on his sufferance."

"That's terrible, Ayden. I'm sorry you had to endure that."

"I survived. And I don't want to end our fun evening on a sour note," Ayden said. "Plus, it's late and

I'd like to get some rest so I'm ready for work tomorrow."

"You don't intend on going to the office, do you?"

Ayden shook his head. "No, not just yet. I'll work from home. At least until I get the hang of those." He nodded toward the crutches lying against a nearby chair.

"Those are easy. I taught Raven how to use them when she broke her leg in middle school."

"Have you spoken to your sister since the baptism?" Ayden inquired.

Maya greeted him with an icy stare. "I thought we were forgoing heavy talk?"

"I was just curious. I know how much she meant to you."

"My sister used to mean everything to me, but as you know, times have changed. We've spoken about my mom's care, but that's about it. You mind if we change the subject?"

"Okay," Ayden said. "I was just trying to be there for you like you've been there for me."

She offered him a smile. "Thank you, and I'm sorry if I bit your head off. I appreciate you caring. It's been a long night, and I'm going so you can get some sleep," Maya said. "I think you've done enough for today."

"I had fun. I can't remember the last time I honestly said that, so thank you." He leaned over and wrapped his arms around her in a hug. It should have been quick, but it lasted a little longer than was necessary. Maya felt her nipples instantly harden into bullets. Had he noticed she was turned on by a simple embrace? When he released her and she glanced up at him, Maya's heart stopped.

He'd noticed. His eyes were liquid, bottomless and filled with desire. She heard his breathing change ever so slightly and a throb of awareness coiled through her. He smiled and ran the back of his fingers down her cheek, and she shuddered. How had they gone from the friend zone to a heat flare in a matter of seconds?

"Ayden…" She didn't get the chance to utter another word because he closed the gap between them and sealed his mouth hungrily over hers. Maya responded to his kiss as every ounce of pent-up frustration from spending the day with him surged through her. She moaned and opened her mouth up to the onslaught of his kiss. She was just as eager as he was to taste, to lick and to twine her tongue with his. She drew him closer and he pushed her backward. Maya felt the pillows at her head as his torso pressed against hers, crushing her breasts against his magnificent bare chest.

Their mouths and bodies aligned perfectly and Maya parted her lips, inviting him in. Ayden took the cue and delved deeper. He took his time exploring, stroking his tongue back and forth against hers.

"This needs to come off," he said, and began tugging at the hem of her sweater. She obliged and tossed the offending garment over her head, revealing her breasts. Moaning, she captured his lips in a savage kiss, clattering her teeth against his as she sought more. Understanding her need, Ayden drew her closer against his body, settling her against his impressive erection. Maya tilted her hips back and forth and began rubbing shamelessly against his rigid length.

"Ayden…" she moaned.

His sizzling eyes sought hers and held. Then he began thrusting upward to meet her hip rolls. A fierce longing gripped Maya's insides. She knew she should slow things down, think about her actions, but she was powerless to fight the carnal desire he incited in her. She wanted to remove every stitch of her clothing and let Ayden make love to her, but she knew it would mean more to her than him. For him, it would just be a release and he'd treat her the same as before.

He sought her face with his hands and brought her closer, diving in to kissing her more thoroughly. Maya could feel herself losing control especially when he pushed his hips forward and ground his erection against her. And when she felt his hands at the zipper of her slim jeans, she didn't stop him. One of his hands snaked lower inside and she laced her fingers with his to guide him to her nub. When he dipped inside her and began stroking her inner walls, Maya was lost as pure pleasure raced through her.

Soon she was gasping and trembling and her muscles clutched his fingers as her climax rolled over her in waves.

"Did that feel good?" Ayden whispered as his lips left her mouth to nuzzle at her neck.

His words woke her up from the haze of desire she'd been under. Embarrassment flushed over her at how wantonly she'd behaved with him. She sat upright, pulling on her sweater as she went.

"Maya?"

"Please don't!" she exclaimed, scooting off the bed. "This...this should never have gotten this far. I told you it was a mistake for me to come here." She ran for the safety and cover of her bedroom. With a sprained ankle, Ayden wouldn't be chasing after her. She had to get some distance and figure out how she'd let the situation get so out of control.

Ten

Frustrated, Ayden sat upright, staring at the door Maya had just run through. Jesus! He rubbed his head. He'd really done it this time. The kiss in his office had been one thing, but tonight they'd had such a wonderful evening together talking, watching television and playing board games that it made Ayden realize just how much he wanted Maya. The heat between them was off the charts, so much so neither of them could deny the sparks when they were in such close quarters.

So he'd kissed her, not thinking about the complications of his actions. The sight of her half-naked body had jolted him. She was so beautiful, from her soft brown skin to her small breasts. She was exquisite and all he wanted to do was slake his thirst for her. Taste her very essence. He wanted to take those dark nipples into his mouth, to sink into her slick heat and let the passion between them explode. But he hadn't gotten the chance because Maya had run away from him *again*.

He wanted to go after her and bring her back to his bed, but he couldn't. Maya was skittish and he didn't blame her. He'd messed up last time when he'd appeared unaffected by their night together even though he'd been far from it. In fact, the desire he'd felt had scared him and he'd tried to marginalize it, brushing it off as good sex and nothing more.

It was certainly the best he'd ever had. And he wanted more. More of Maya. But how did he convince her to explore this side of their relationship when he'd hurt her before? Add the fact that he wasn't keeping the promise he'd made to her to keep their relationship professional and no wonder she was upset. Usually Ayden was a man of his word. He prided himself on it. But when it came to Maya, he didn't think with a level head. He'd been so convinced that night five years ago had been a fluke that he'd simply imagined how intense the attraction between them had been, but he was wrong. Years ago, he'd deceived himself, refusing to admit how much she meant to him, and now look at where they were.

Ayden glanced at the clock. It was after midnight and he was in no mood to sleep. His mind was racing, as he kept reliving the moment she'd come and the sounds she'd made when his fingers had been buried inside her. Jesus! Didn't she understand that she couldn't fight this attraction any more than he could? Because as sure as the sun rose in the morning, it was inevitable that they would fall into bed again. The chemistry between them would no longer be denied. It had probably always been there. Five years ago, they'd opened that door and there was no going back. Ayden had found the one and only woman who made him want to go back on his word.

Maya awoke the next morning knowing what she had to do. She had to leave Ayden, the job, Austin, all of it. Money be damned. She'd figure out a way to help pay her mother's cancer treatment bills. She was bright, and qualified assistants were always in high demand. She would find a job.

Throwing the covers off, Maya went to the bathroom. After brushing her teeth, showering and dressing, she packed up her minimal toiletries. Heading back to the bedroom, she pulled the suitcase out of the closet. She hadn't had time to unpack because she'd been so focused on caring for Ayden yesterday. Maya placed the luggage by the door and paused because she wanted to smell the flowers outside her balcony one last time before she left. When Ayden had said she could make herself comfortable, she'd chosen the room above the gardens. Opening the door, she walked to the railing and looked out over the colorful plants in full bloom, taking in the fragrance wafting in the air around her.

Her arrangement with Ayden was untenable. She couldn't continue doing the same thing and expecting a different result. Ayden was her Achilles' heel and she had to face it that being his nursemaid would undoubtedly have her winding up in his bed. Maya accepted that she had no willpower when it came to resisting him. Callie was right. She was in over her head.

She heard a creak behind her and turned to find Ayden on crutches behind her. Maya didn't speak and turned back around to stare at the garden.

"Maya, I recognize that last night the situation got out of control."

"You mean that boundary we crossed, that *you* said wouldn't happen again?"

She heard his sharp intake of breath. It wasn't fair to blame him entirely for what had happened. She'd played an active role. She whirled around. "I'm sorry. That was unfair."

He shook his head. "No, you're right. I promised to keep my hands to myself, but failed miserably. And if we're being honest, I can't promise that I'm not going to touch you, not kiss you, and not make love to you."

All of Maya's tingly parts came alive at his bold declaration. "So then you're in agreement that we can't work together and it's best we terminate this agreement."

"Far from it."

"Pardon?" She didn't understand. He'd just said that he wasn't going to keep his promise for their relationship to remain professional.

"I think we need to acknowledge there is something between us and *act* on it. Stop denying it exists and just see where it goes."

"Straight to your bed," she countered. "Because we both know where it will lead."

"And is it so wrong that we enjoy each other?" Ayden asked, hopping toward her until they were a few feet apart. "Don't you think it's high time we started acting like adults and admit we're attracted to each other?"

"Ayden…"

"You want me. Don't you?"

Maya lowered her gaze. She couldn't believe they were having this conversation. Right now. He was putting everything out in the open and pulling no punches. When she didn't answer, she felt him throw the crutches to the ground and move over to the railing until he was inches from her face.

"I dare you to say you don't."

Maya rolled her eyes upward. "Yes, I want you. There. Are you happy? I admit it."

"No, not really because you're too far away from me to kiss you properly."

Maya leaned over and Ayden rewarded her with a hot, deep kiss. She moaned softly, opened her mouth, allowed his tongue to dip inside and mate with hers. *What was she doing?* Maya wrenched herself away and when he leaned in again, she put her hand against his hard chest. "Are you sure about this?"

"Yes. Don't deny us this pleasure when we both want this."

She did want him more than she had any other

man, and he was offering her the opportunity to have unfettered access to him. But what did it all mean? What happened once he tired of her?

"Stop thinking, Maya. For once, just feel, allow yourself to let go and be *mine*."

His words startled her. Be his. They'd only been together once and it had been the most amazing sexual experience of her life. If she allowed herself to go there again, Maya was afraid she'd never be the same again. The first time she'd been completely devastated and had had to move away because she couldn't stand to be near him. What would happen this time?

"Come away with me."

She frowned in consternation. "Where?"

"To Jamaica. You were right. I never take a vacation and now, with this bum ankle, it's a prime opportunity to take some time off and explore us." He wound his hands around her neck and pulled her closer, bringing her into his air space. He leaned his forehead against hers. "Come away with me."

"I don't know, Ayden." She pulled away. "You're moving too fast. You want me to fly to Jamaica at a moment's notice? I have responsibilities now. You know I want to be here for my mother's next treatment."

"Of course, I understand that. It would be a short getaway. Plenty of time for you to get back, but enough time for us to discover our feelings in paradise without any outside influences."

Maya was torn. She did want to go with Ayden, but she was also afraid to jump into the deep end of the ocean without a life vest. Even though he'd admitted his desire for her, Ayden had the power to hurt her because she still had unresolved feelings for him. Feelings that went deeper than lust. Yet, if she didn't take this opportunity she would always wonder what could have been.

"All right, I'll go with you."

Maya couldn't believe she was on a recliner in a living room–style cabin of a private plane on her way to Montego Bay with Ayden. Once she'd agreed, Ayden had contacted his pilot to file a flight plan. In her wildest dreams, she would never have imagined that he would want to spend time alone with her or that she'd readily agree. But one devilish yet sinfully sexy look from him had her abandoning her principles and packing a suitcase for Jamaica. And she knew full well what was in store during their stay—mind-blowing, toe-curling sex the likes of which she'd never experienced except with him.

Maya was both excited and terrified. She was by no means a virgin, but she'd only been with a handful of men. And none of them had ever made her feel the way Ayden did. One look, one touch from him set her on fire. She didn't want to disappoint him.

A lump formed in her throat. She regarded him from across the aisle where he lay sprawled out on the couch with his ankle up, playing with his tablet. He seemed perfectly content, as if he didn't have a care in the world. Was he used to whisking women away on getaways to paradise so he could wine and dine them and take them to bed? Or maybe there would be no wining and dining, just sex. Full stop.

She hazarded a glance at him and found his eyes on her. "What are you worrying about, Maya? I hope you're not regretting your decision to come with me."

She shook her head. "I'm just wondering what you have in store for me."

He chuckled, showing off his winsome smile and perfect white teeth. "If you're asking if I intend to let you come up for air after I've had my wicked way with you, the answer is yes. We're going to Jamaica on vacation. I may not be able to do everything like climbing Dunn's River Falls, but we can certainly take in the sights and enjoy the culture."

Maya smiled brightly. "All right, that sounds good."

"You're too far away over there. Why don't you come over here." He gave her a wink and patted the empty seat beside him.

"Ayden Stewart, I have no intention of becoming a member of the mile-high club. Plus, the crew is just in the other room." She inclined her head toward the front of the cabin where the pilots and flight attendant were assembled.

"I promise to be good."

"I highly doubt that."

"Come here," he commanded. The tone of his voice had Maya rising from her seat and moving to him, but she stopped a few inches away from him. It forced Ayden to sit upright, grasp her arm and haul her forward. "This is much better," he said when she was in his lap. "And this will be even better." He lowered his head and brushed his lips across hers. She was fast becoming addicted to his kisses. He used everything in his arsenal to make her his willing captive.

When he finally lifted his head, he smiled as he looked at her. "You look thoroughly kissed. Every man will know that you're with me."

He sat her upright and for the rest of the flight wouldn't let her leave his side. Maya supposed she should be flattered by all this attention, but what happened at the end of their vacation? Where did they go from there? She shook her head. She wouldn't think of the future, only the here and now with Ayden for the scant time she had with him.

They arrived in Jamaica later that afternoon and were met on the tarmac by a limousine. A driver took care of their luggage and his crutches while Ayden leaned on Maya for support to help him to the limo. Soon they were leaving Montego Bay and heading through the countryside. Maya peered out the window taking in the sights of the island country.

"You look like a kid in a candy store," Ayden said.

Maya turned away from the window. "I'm sorry, am I being too gauche? I've only been out of the country once during spring break when I let Callie talk me into going to Cancun."

"And how did that go?"

"Terrible. Callie was wasted half the time and when she wasn't, she was curled up next to several guys. I spent much of the time reading on the beach.

The best part of that vacation was the fact that I was of legal drinking age and could partake in the cocktails."

Ayden stared at her for several long moments. "Have you ever done anything out of your comfort zone?"

"This," she responded. "I'm running off to an island to have an affair with my boss."

"Is that all I am to you—your boss?" Ayden asked.

His question startled her. She hadn't meant to offend him. If she had, it was a bad start to their journey. "No, of course not." She moved away from the window. "I'm sorry, you're more than just my boss." She took a deep breath and said what she truly felt. "You're about to become my lover."

He grinned and the light returned to his eyes. "That's right. And I intend to ensure I satisfy your every need."

"I can't wait."

They arrived at a beautiful villa built on the side of the mountain. It was the epitome of romance. The home was surrounded by long clinging vines, bougainvillea, fragrant flowers and dense green trees. There wasn't another house for miles. They would be secluded in this love nest. Tucked away from the world. Just the two of them.

Once their bags were taken inside, Ayden grabbed the crutches and showed Maya the grounds. "You've stayed here before?" she asked.

He nodded. "I come here sometimes when I need to be alone."

Maya wondered if he'd ever made peace with what happened, but chose not to ask. She just followed behind him. The inside of the home was white and clean with modern furnishings. The large kitchen and living area were open to the great outdoors which overlooked a terrace that had a luxurious infinity pool for their use. "I can't wait to slip into my bathing suit and get in."

"Who says you need a bikini?" Ayden replied, "We're the only ones here, Maya. You can feel comfortable in your birthday suit."

She turned away and began walking down the corridor to see the rest of the home. He wanted her to walk out in the open completely nude? She could never do that. She'd feel too self-conscious. Raven had always had the rocking body with curves for days that men liked, while Maya had always had a slightly boyish figure. Thank God, she'd finally gotten boobs.

Ayden caught up with her at the master suite, which housed a raised platform bed with a silky duvet in deep red and loads of cream pillows strewn over it. Swaths of fabric hung from the ceiling, draping the bed. They were gauzy and sexy. It clearly wasn't a bed made for sleeping.

"Maya!"

"Hmm?"

"Sit." He motioned to the bed and Maya took a seat so they could be eye to eye. "You have nothing to be ashamed or embarrassed about. You have a beautiful body."

"You don't have to say that, Ayden. I know that I'm not like the curvaceous women you usually date."

He cupped her chin, tilting her head so he could peer into her eyes. "Maya, I love your body."

"You do?"

"Yes, and I can't wait to show you just how much."

"When?" she asked expectantly, eagerly.

He gave her a wolfish grin. "Later, after dinner."

"Promise?"

"Oh, it's a promise I intend to keep all night long."

Eleven

Ayden ignored the jolt of arousal that had been surging through him from the moment they'd arrived. He wanted to give Maya the romantic evening she deserved rather than immediately throwing her down on the bed and thrusting inside her wet heat until she called out his name. It was crazy to think that for years he'd been blind to her beauty until that night five years ago opened his eyes. Ayden always had boundaries and each person had their proper place, but he'd been unable to put Maya back into the box he'd had her in. Instead, all their time together was marked by sexual tension and awareness.

Tonight was no different. After arriving, they'd both showered—*separately*—and were now in the living room having a drink before dinner. Ayden had arranged for a local catering company to drop off meals for them during their stay. A candlelight dinner was set up on the patio along with a bucket of champagne so he and Maya could eat underneath the stars. When they were ready, all they had to do was pull the food out from the warmer on the counter. Soup was in a heated container nearby and salad plates were already in place.

But he wasn't sure he wanted dinner. He wanted to devour Maya. Her beautiful dark brown hair was stylish, sleek and straight. She'd changed into a print sundress with spaghetti straps that stopped at the knee, giving him an unfettered view of her long legs.

It wasn't easy navigating, but he managed to pull out her chair. "Thank you," Maya said once she was seated.

Ayden shuffled to the other side, tossing down his crutches. "You're looking exceptionally lovely this evening, Maya."

She blushed. "Thank you."

"Would you like some champagne?"

"Love some."

He took care of pouring the bubbly into their glasses and, once filled, leaned both elbows over and held up his flute. "A toast."

"To us."

"And unexplored territories," Ayden finished, sipping his champagne.

Maya drank her champagne, regarding him from under mascara-coated lashes. He noticed she wasn't wearing much makeup and he liked that about her;

she was comfortable being herself. He wanted her to feel that way, but he sensed her tension from across the table.

So he began talking about the fun things they were going to see and do in Jamaica while he ladled soup into the bowls on the table. "I've hired a tour guide for the day after tomorrow. Thought he could show us around the island. You can take some photos."

She smiled as she accepted her soup bowl. "I'm looking forward to it. Hopefully, we'll get to eat some authentic jerk chicken. I hear Jamaica has some of the best."

"I didn't realize you liked spicy food."

"Then you need to catch up on all things Maya. Starting with how I like my pizza."

Ayden appreciated this feisty side of Maya, and over the next hour as they tucked into their dinner of Caribbean-style fish with grilled pineapple, shrimp and vanilla-rum butter sauce, he learned even more about her. He knew she loved running but didn't know she listened to Audible during her runs. Or that she had a fear of heights due to falling off the monkey bars when she was six years old. In his prior relationships, if he could call them that, he'd never taken the time to get to know their likes and dislikes, but Maya made him want to go deeper, know more.

By the end of the evening, they'd adjourned to a large chaise and removed their shoes to stargaze. They'd imbibed the entire bottle of champagne, along with a fair share of wine with their meal. They were both feeling relaxed, so it was only natural when Ayden leaned over and brushed his lips across Maya's. Hers were soft and sweet like the creamy custard of the crème brûlée they'd had earlier for dessert.

She tasted so good he dipped his head for another taste. Maya wound her arms around his neck and he pressed his body against hers. Feeling her against him was electrifying and he slid his hands down her bare arms to her breasts. He caressed the small mounds and felt her nipples pebble to his touch. And when she shuddered, he knew Maya was ready to take their relationship to the next level.

He rose up on one arm and looked down at her. "Why did you stop?" she asked, looking up at him in bewilderment.

"I just want you to be sure, Maya."

"I'm sure, Ayden. I want you. So stop talking and make love to me." She clasped his head and brought his mouth down on hers. He tried to keep it gentle, but the kiss deepened and desire bloomed. He wanted to explore her, taste every inch of her. His mouth left hers and found a path to her shoulders. He kissed the soft blades, sliding the straps of her sundress down as he went until her dress was lowered to her waist and he could feast his eyes on her breasts.

He bent down and closed his mouth over one round globe. Maya nearly jackknifed off the chaise as he sucked it deep into his mouth, swirling the rock-hard tip with his tongue. He alternated between sucking and licking and tugging the sensitive nipple with his teeth, causing Maya to squirm underneath him. The fact that she was so turned-on pleased him tremendously and he intended on giving her a lot more pleasure. He splayed his hand across her stomach to keep her down, so he could lean over and palm the other breast and give it the same ministration.

While his mouth played havoc with her upper body, his hands roamed lower, aiming for the place between her legs. His fingers slid underneath her dress, which had shifted up to her waist with all her squirming. He snatched the tiny scrap of fabric from her hips and tossed it aside, then plunged deep inside. Ayden found her deliciously hot and wet. He was thrilled with the knowledge that she was ready for him. His groin tightened in anticipation of what was to come.

"Ayden," Maya cried out when his fingers teased her, stroking in and out of her core.

"I want to taste you," he said gruffly. He moved lower to kiss her abdomen and stomach until he came to her hips and thighs. He splayed them open with his arms, pushing them wider to make room for what he wanted to do. He teased her first not giving her what she wanted. He licked the inside of both of her thighs, the back of her knees, even kissed her feet before he came back to her core. He licked the seam and Maya let out a sob of pleasure that only made Ayden want more. His tongue slid in farther, teasing the sensitive nub with soft flicks and licks. Her legs began to shake and she began to shiver uncontrollably.

She was close.

"Please," she begged him. Her moans and mews were driving Ayden crazy. He knew what she wanted, but he wasn't about to give it to her. Not yet. If he did, he wouldn't be able to hold himself together and would climax almost immediately because that's how hard his erection was. He needed to sate her first. Otherwise, if he took her now, it would be over too quick.

"Easy, love," he whispered, and returned to feverishly stroking her with his tongue until her entire body spasmed and she clutched around him. Her honeyed taste filled his senses and he lapped her until she eventually subsided.

Maya couldn't believe she'd just let Ayden make love to her out in the open. She'd always been somewhat of a prude. It was like she was outside her body, but couldn't stop herself. The man made her wanton and greedy for whatever he had in store. And if she allowed herself to think about it, she'd stop, and she didn't want to. She was enjoying being with Ayden and exploring this side of herself.

"Are you all right?" he asked, glancing up at her as he eased upward to kiss her.

She could taste herself on his lips. It was heady stuff. She ached to touch him, but she wanted to do so when they were skin to skin. She rose onto her knees and quickly threw off her sundress, tossing it to the floor.

Ayden grinned as she sat before him, completely and unabashedly naked while he was still fully clothed. "So beautiful." His eyes darkened and Maya felt the words through every part of her.

She leaned forward and began unbuttoning his

shirt. He shrugged it off his broad shoulders, bringing into view his beautiful torso along with his muscular biceps and trim waist. Her fingers tingled to touch more. She moved to his belt, loosening each loop, until finally she could unzip him. He stood and dropped his pants and they fell to the floor by her dress. Then he worked off his boxers to reveal the most spectacular erection she'd ever seen.

He was beautiful and *large*.

She would gladly take all of him inside her because she'd wanted this for so long. She hadn't thought it would ever be possible to be with Ayden again, yet here she was. He crawled onto the chaise beside her, covering her body with his, and Maya lost all coherent thought except that she was exactly where she wanted to be. In the moonlit darkness, Maya felt it was safe to say exactly what she wanted. "Please, Ayden."

"Please what?"

"Make love to me."

He gathered her in his arms and claimed her mouth. His fingertips caressed her all over with feather-soft strokes, up and down her side and then lower until his fingers slid along her crease. He teased her core, testing her yet again, making sure she was wet. And when he locked gazes with her, she knew he was seeing if she had any last-minute regrets. But she didn't have any. Then she watched as he retrieved a condom from his pants pocket and sheathed himself.

Soon she felt the ridge of his shaft, notching at her entrance. He eased forward inch by delicious inch and she gasped. But she wanted him even deeper and lifted her knees to help guide him in farther. He braced himself on his elbows and in one fell swoop surged inside her.

"Oh, yes," Maya moaned. It felt right to be joined with Ayden this way.

"You feel so good, Maya. And so tight," he panted as he began moving inside her. "Why did I ever think I could resist you?"

Maya didn't have an answer because she too had been denying the pull between them. But he'd been right. It was inevitable that they would end up like this. And so she gave into the moment, wrapping her ankles around his back and lifting her hips to move to the rhythm he set. Ayden flexed his powerful body and she sensed he was struggling for control because he began thrusting frantically. She parted her thighs wider, wanting him to fill her as completely as only he could.

"Maya…" He rasped out her name and his hold tightened around her as he pumped faster and faster.

"Yes," she cried as tension began building inside her. She could feel her body begin to tremble and she grabbed his buttocks and clutched him closer to her. And when he pulled back, only to thrust in again, she greedily met him as he pushed their pace. When her climax hit, she became undone and screamed his name.

He continued pounding into her until, moments later, she heard a loud groan rip from deep inside him and he fell on top of her. Maya tried to suck in air, but it was impossible. She gasped for breath as he rolled to her side.

Maya lay still, afraid to look at him, staring at the stars overhead. Had he felt the intensity of their coupling as she had? They'd been frenetic, more intense than five years ago. Yet it had been a totally sublime experience that she couldn't wait to relive over and over throughout their days in Jamaica.

"That was over much too quick," Ayden said softly from beside her.

With a small grin, she turned to him. "It was sensational."

"I'm sorry. I'm usually more in control, but with you…" His voice trailed off.

"With me what?"

"I can't seem to find it anymore."

She was happy that he felt he could be honest with her. "I've felt the same way for a long time."

"How long?"

"C'mon, Ayden, are you saying you didn't notice that I pined for you for years before I met Thomas? Maybe even after…"

He rose up on an elbow to look at her. "No, no, I didn't. I've always been aware of you, Maya—" he stroked her cheek "—but you were always so composed and buttoned up. And then when you came to me upset and brokenhearted, I don't know, something snapped and all I wanted to do was make you feel good. Special. Adored."

"You did that then. And now," she whispered as the warmth of his words enveloped her. She was eager for him to tell her more. Instead, he reached for her, closing the gap and sealing her mouth hungrily with his. She reciprocated, responding to him with abandoned enthusiasm. His arms wrapped tightly around her and Maya felt the hard ridge of his shaft against her middle. She couldn't believe he'd recovered that quickly. Or that she was just as desperate to feel him inside her again.

A maelstrom of unbridled lust and passion that only Ayden could quench took over. She crawled up the length of his body and straddled him, settling against his bulge. Ayden's gaze was dark and intense and filled with desire. He reached for yet another condom and rolled it on. She watched him, spellbound. And when he grasped her hips firmly, she sank down on him, drawing him in. He filled her in the best possible way. "Yes," she purred.

She enthusiastically began grinding hard against him, eager to feel his powerful body pressing against hers. Her hair fell into her face, but she didn't care. She put her hands on his chest for leverage and adjusted the angle, taking him even deeper inside her. And when she found the right rhythm, she rode him.

"Damn it, Maya." Ayden stared up at her, his skin glistening with sweat. She could feel him trying to slow down the pace, but she kept undulating against him. That's when he began to devour her, holding her more tightly as he nudged his hips higher, thrusting harder and faster into her. When her orgasm struck, her back arched like a bow, and only seconds later, a loud guttural groan burst from his beautiful lips. He thrust one final time and her entire chest constricted as yet another tidal wave of pleasure surged through her. All Maya could see was a flash of lightning as she closed her eyes and fell forward, drifting into another dimension.

Twelve

Maya stirred awake the next morning on the platform bed in the master suite as light streamed through the windows. How had she gotten here? Then she recalled that sometime during the night, Ayden had scooped her into his arms and carried her to the bedroom where he'd proceeded to make her come again and again. But where was he now? When she glanced over at his side of the bed, he was gone and the sheets were cool to the touch.

Last night had been an incredible night of lovemaking and snuggling next to Ayden. He'd been voracious in his appetite for her. Her underutilized muscles were slammed while several intimate areas felt sore, but she welcomed that if it meant Ayden wanted her as much as she wanted him.

Determined to go find him, she sat up, threw off the covers and went in search of something to wear. She was rummaging through her suitcase when Ayden returned carrying a tray laden with food and coffee mugs.

"Where do you think you're going?" he asked.

"To find you." Maya grabbed her silk robe and slung her arms through it, knotting it at the waist.

"Did I say you were allowed to get dressed?" Ayden asked as he laid the tray on the bed and took a seat.

She grinned. "I can't very well walk around naked."

"Why not?"

Maya flushed. She didn't answer him; instead, she walked toward the bed and sat beside him. "What do you have here?"

"Some omelets, toast, fresh squeezed orange juice and coffee."

"You made all this?"

"Oh, heck no, the catering company stopped by this morning."

"Did they? I didn't hear them."

He grinned. "That's because you were exhausted."

"I wonder why."

He rolled to his side and leaned over to kiss her. "I can think of a number of reasons, but you need to eat. And I'll draw you a bath. I suspect you're a bit sore this morning." He searched her eyes for confirmation. "We, were, um, very vigorous last night."

Maya flushed. He was right. He hadn't been gentle, but she hadn't wanted him to be. Nevertheless, she'd never spoken so openly about intimacy with another man. "Thank you. That would be lovely."

He hopped off the bed and headed for the en suite while Maya continued nibbling on toast and the delicious Denver omelet. She heard the tap running and smiled at his thoughtfulness. When she was done eating and Ayden hadn't returned she went to the bathroom. He had not only drawn a bath, but he was in it.

"Are you coming in or do I have to come and get you?"

"That won't be necessary," Maya said, relieving herself of her robe and sinking into the steaming water. She leaned back against Ayden, pressing her backside against his shaft. He was semi-erect, but that was quickly changing. She opened for him, letting him take any liberties he chose, but he didn't. Instead, he washed her thoroughly and then eventually swaddled her in a towel and carried her back to the bed.

Maya was a bit disappointed. She'd thought he would gather her against his chest so she could straddle him and go for another round, but instead, he laid her down on the bed. Desperate not to lose the connection, she circled her arms around his neck. He kissed her then, openmouthed, with such raw passion that her brain short-circuited. Heat pooled at her core, making her want him all over again. "Ayden…"

"Hmm…" He'd moved from her mouth and was nibbling at the sensitive spots on her nape and neck. When he dipped his tongue inside her ear, Maya moaned.

"Feel good?"

"Yes…"

"I'd like you to feel even better." He shifted down her body and Maya parted her legs, letting him in.

He glanced up, his eyes locking with hers momentarily before he began to pleasure her. He teased her with his tongue and fingers, arousing her so much so that she thrashed and begged him to take her, but he didn't. Instead, he licked her until her orgasm struck hot and fierce and she came apart. Her entire body trembled and he kissed through the aftershocks until lethargy took over and she closed her eyes.

But as she drifted off, the truth hit her hard in the chest. Maya had allowed herself these moments to enjoy Ayden and all he could offer because deep down she knew it wouldn't last.

Ayden hadn't made any promises. He'd only offered her this week, this moment in time when it was just the two of them away from the world. She'd taken it and she wouldn't surrender to regret now.

She was here in Jamaica with Ayden, the man she loved. Oh yes, that was the truth. There was no denying it.

She loved him.

Ayden stared down at Maya's sleeping figure. Her mass of hair was spread across the pillows like a fan. He gently lifted a strand and breathed in the fresh citrus scent. It smelled like Maya, and his chest felt tight and his breathing became harder. He rubbed his forehead.

He'd thought coming to Jamaica would help clear

up this insatiable need he felt for Maya, but it appeared he'd only stoked the flames. Waking up with Maya by his side should have been alarming because he typically never stayed the night with other lovers. Once his lust was sated, he left and returned to his own home to sleep. But, with Maya, he felt like he was home. And when he'd turned to her during the night, she'd welcomed him with open arms, all too eager to please.

And she had pleased him immensely.

With each orgasm, her tight, slender body had blown his mind into a million pieces. He'd watched her responses, heard her cries and moans as he'd extracted every ounce of pleasure he could from her pert breasts to the thatch of hair between her thighs. She was his fantasy come to life and he'd made sure to taste every inch of her.

Just now, he'd wanted to take her again and she'd been willing, but he'd needed to regain some composure. He felt off his game. Felt as if he was diving into the deep end of the ocean without knowing how to swim. They would have to get out of this house tonight. If they didn't, Ayden feared he'd keep her naked and writhing on the bed for the entire length of their stay.

Eventually, Maya did awake and he arranged for them to go to Rick's Café, one of the famous bars in Jamaica. They arrived before sunset so they could see the brave souls willing to jump off the highest cliff into the Caribbean. They'd dressed casually for the night out; he was wearing linen trousers and a matching button-down shirt while Maya had opted for a filmy dress that left her shoulders bare.

"We're here," the driver announced when the limo stopped.

"Ready for a fun night?" Ayden asked, squeezing Maya's hand, which had been resting in his for the entire drive from the villa.

"Absolutely."

The well-known bar was alive with activity, full of bikini-clad and bare-chested patrons. After a well-slipped tip, the host was able to find them a table overlooking the West Cliffs. The view was spectacular, and Ayden was looking forward to the sunset as well as time spent with the woman across from him.

"This is great, Ayden. I'd heard about this place and always wanted to come."

"Are you feeling adventurous?" He inclined his head toward the top of the cliff divers were jumping from.

Maya shook her head. "No, thank you. I'll leave it to the daredevils. But I'll cheer them on from here."

"My kind of gal."

He appreciated Maya even more when instead of ordering a cocktail, she got a Red Stripe like a local and indulged in jerk chicken and Jamaican beef patties. The woman was full of surprises. He doubted any of the well-coiffed women he usually dated would be caught dead in an establishment like this. For them, it had to be five-star all the way, but Maya was content with just being normal. Ayden didn't realize just how much he'd been missing out on until now.

They didn't stay and close down Rick's Café. After watching the colorful and vibrant sunset and dancing hip to hip to reggae music from the live band, Ayden was horny as hell. When Maya had put her rear to his groin and begun grinding her hips to the rhythmical music, he'd been in both heaven and hell. Hell because he was getting turned on by a dance in front of too many people and heaven because it would take hours to get back to the villa so they would have plenty of time to enjoy each other in the limo.

After finding the condom in his wallet, he knew he wasn't even going to try. Once they were seated in the limo, he hauled Maya into his lap and crushed her mouth to his. He indulged himself in her with long sweeps of his tongue, thrusting and stroking until eventually he had to come up for air. All he could think about was touching her, kissing her. He leaned his forehead against hers.

"I want you," he murmured.

"We're in a limo." The blacked-out divider had been lifted as soon as they'd entered.

"I don't care." He lifted her so she was straddling him. Then he ran his hands through her hair and brought her mouth forward to his. And when he'd tasted his fill, he bent his head to suck her through the fabric of her dress. He reveled when she arched to meet him, pressing her nipple into his mouth so he could take a nip. Ayden reached underneath the dress to find the thong, the only piece of underwear he knew she was wearing. He was delighted to find it damp with desire and, with a tug, ripped it from her body. Then he plunged a finger inside her.

"Ayden…"

He stopped her cries by closing his mouth over hers and let his hands do all the talking. He began feverishly stroking her and she bucked against him, her breathing coming in short gasps, but he had no intention of letting her climax without him. He reached between them and tugged at the zipper on his trousers until he got himself free, then lifting his hips, he shoved them down with one hand while holding Maya in the other.

"Maya," he groaned, and handed her the condom. "Put it on."

She looked at him, her eyes glazed with desire, and complied. Once he was sheathed, he kissed her again and thrust inside her.

"Oh, baby, you feel so good," he said, before withdrawing slightly and slamming back in again. He repeated the process over and over and Maya lifted her hips to meet him as he went as deep as he could. But this couldn't be just about him and his release. Slipping his hand between their bodies, he found her sweet spot and pressed his thumb there. Maya's entire body began to shake, her muscles contracting around him.

Ayden was lost and all he could do was continue pumping inside her until he felt the familiar tension build in his body. He stiffened and then exploded inside of her, triggering yet another orgasm for Maya. She collapsed against him, clutching his shoulders and circling her arms around his neck.

Neither of them spoke for the remainder of the

drive. They just tidied themselves up as best they could until the driver eventually pulled up in front of the villa. Ayden glanced over at Maya. Her hair was unkempt and her dress was wrinkled with damp spots at her nipples. There was no denying she looked as if she'd been made love to. And even though he'd just had her, Ayden wanted her again.

He was in big trouble. If this was how he felt after a few days with Maya, how was he going to feel when their short time in Jamaica was over? He was quickly losing his head to this beautiful, amazing woman, and it scared the living daylights out of him.

Maya sat across from Ayden as they played a game of dominos on the deck outside the villa. She'd enjoyed these lazy days in Jamaica with Ayden. Waking up and going to sleep, making love or just lounging by the pool.

When she had time, she'd called her sister to check in on their mother. They didn't talk long, only enough for Raven to inform her that Sophia was lethargic and nauseous, but otherwise hanging in there. Maya wished there was more she could do, but they had to allow the chemo to do what it was designed for. After the call, she was down in the dumps, so she was especially excited when Ayden had told her they would tour the island and visit Dunn's River Falls.

Ayden hadn't been able to climb the falls with a bum ankle, but he'd waited for her at the bottom while she'd soldiered up the cliff. Afterward, however, he'd been sore and achy from the hiking and she'd had to give him a foot rub and put him to sleep. That hadn't lasted long and he'd woken up in the middle of the night as hungry for her as he'd been that night in the back seat of the limo. She blushed thinking of the encounter.

She lifted her fingers to her lips, recalling the feel of his mouth and how magical his kisses were.

"And what are you thinking about?" Ayden asked as he moved another domino.

"Oh, nothing. What are we going to do on our last night here?"

"Anything you want."

"How about we find the nearest hot spot and hang out with the locals?"

"You sure?"

"Why not? Could be fun."

"I'm game if you are."

Just then Ayden's cell phone buzzed beside him. He glanced down at it but didn't answer, as he'd done for several days now. Although she wanted to ask him who was trying so urgently to reach him, she was afraid to delve too deep.

"Important call?"

He shook his head. "Yes...no...maybe so."

"Which is it?"

Ayden shrugged again and she could see his shoulders stiffen as if he didn't want to answer, but he did. "It's my sister, Fallon. She's been trying to reach me to convince me to help her."

"But you can't."

"*Won't* would be a more accurate word." Ayden made another move. "I won."

Maya glanced down and, indeed, he had, but her

mind hadn't been on the game. It had been on him. "Maybe you should talk to her."

"It won't change my mind, Maya. I'll give the Stewart family exactly what they gave me. Nothing. I owe them no allegiance."

"True, but she is your sister."

"In blood only. And why are you pushing this anyway?" He glared at her. "You more than anyone know how my mother and I were treated by Henry Stewart."

Maya was surprised by the icy glare Ayden was giving her. She knew it was a touchy subject, but she was trying to help. She cared deeply for this man and his well-being. "Yes, of course I do."

"Then why?" he pressed.

"Because…" Her voice trailed off.

"Speak your mind, Maya. You obviously have something to say."

"I just want you to be happy, and settling things with your family might bring you the peace you crave."

"I *am* happy," he replied. He reached across the distance between them, grabbed her arm and pulled her into his lap. "Here with you." He grasped both sides of her face and kissed her hard on the mouth.

Maya could see what he was doing. He was effectively ending the conversation and shutting her out like he always did. And she let him because it was what he needed. But some day—some day soon—there would be a reckoning that he wouldn't be able to turn away from.

Thirteen

About an hour before arriving home in Austin, Ayden looked out the window of his private jet and reflected. He had enjoyed Jamaica and spending time alone with Maya, but it was time for him to get back to work. He'd never been gone this long from Stewart Investments. It was his baby. A dream he'd accomplished on his own with no help from Henry Stewart.

Which was why Fallon's request was so misguided. She had to have known he would turn her down. Ayden had been estranged from the Stewart family for decades. Had it really come as a surprise to her? It must have, because she'd been trying to reach him on and off for the last three days.

He glanced across the cabin at Maya, who was lying on a reclining chair sleeping soundly with her

Kindle in her lap. He'd been banking on having a little fun while airborne and seeing if he could convince her to become a member of the mile-high club. Over this week, she'd not only been an extremely passionate lover, she'd been open to trying new things, like when he'd pulled some silk sashes from his luggage and tied her hands… Christ! He needed to get a grip. They were going back to Austin to work. Now that his ankle was starting to feel better, he wouldn't need any help at home. Maya could go back to her apartment if she wanted. The problem was, he didn't want her to. His emotions had become entangled and he wanted her with him. But for how long? He didn't know, but surely they could figure out something. He sat up straight, frustrated by the circumstances.

She stirred in the recliner and glanced over at him. "How long was I out?"

"Not long." He closed the report he'd been reading on his tablet. "We'll be landing in another hour."

She rubbed the sleep from her eyes. "Great. That will give me time to freshen up."

"You look beautiful, as always."

"If you say so."

"Maya, I would think after a week in Jamaica with me that you know I find you utterly ravishing."

A grin spread across her face. "Yes, I suppose."

"Suppose? Why don't you come over here and I'll convince you."

She shook her head. "Oh, no, you don't. The limo was bad enough, but not the airplane."

He laughed. "All right. You can't blame a man for

trying. So listen. I think we should discuss what happens when we get back."

Maya's eyes grew large and he saw genuine fear in their depths. He would have to tread carefully because he didn't want to hurt her. Not now. Not ever.

"Yes?"

"You're moving in with me."

Her mouth turned down in a frown. "Is that a question or a statement?"

"The latter."

"I don't recall being asked."

"You agreed to take care of me," Ayden replied, annoyed by her response.

"And now you're healed."

"Are you saying you don't want to come back home with me?" Ayden wasn't ready to let her go, not by a long shot. She'd come to mean more to him than just a lover. She was his friend.

"Of course not, but we hadn't really discussed it."

"We're discussing it now." Why was she being so noncommittal? This wasn't like her. Now that the shoe was on the other foot, was she done with him? He couldn't believe that. He'd been with her, he knew Maya cared a great deal about him. Surely this wasn't the end of the road?

She sighed. "Yes, we are. I just wasn't sure of what you wanted. I just assumed that Jamaica was Jamaica, and I would move back to my place."

Ayden couldn't believe he'd misjudged the situation so entirely. Unbuckling his seat belt, he walked over and sat beside Maya. He grasped her delicate hand in his. "I'm sorry if I wasn't clear about what I wanted and how absolutely hot I am for you. I want you to come back with me to my home. Please say that you will."

Maya stared into his hazel eyes. Any girl would jump at the chance to have what he was offering, but she was hesitant. She knew Ayden didn't share her feelings. He hadn't said he was in love with or even that he was falling for her. He'd said he was *hot* for her. Meaning that as long as she was willing to be his bedmate, he'd happily have her. But again her mind went back to that age-old question: *how long?*

"Maya?" He sounded unsure. It saddened her that she was making him feel this way, but she also had to protect her heart.

"Maybe it's best if I go back to the apartment. I mean, you're better now and you don't really need a nursemaid."

"Or a lover?" he asked coldly, pulling his hand away from her and rising to his feet. "Are you saying you've tired of me after one week?"

"No, that's not what I'm saying at all," Maya responded hotly, jumping to her feet. "Don't put words in my mouth, Ayden Stewart."

"Then what? Why are you turning me down? I know it's not because you didn't like the sex. I lost count of your orgasms."

Tears sprang, stinging her eyes. How could he

speak to her this way after the week they'd shared? She spun away from him and began walking to the lavatory, but he called after her. She couldn't face him because she feared he would see the tears fall.

"Maya, wait! I'm sorry. I shouldn't have said that." He reached her with two long strides and caught her at the door. "I'm truly sorry. You didn't deserve that. I guess I don't know how to do this." He rubbed his head in frustration.

"Do what?"

"Be casual with you about sex. You're not like the other women I've been with. You're Maya."

"And that's a bad thing?" Her voice cracked when she looked at him.

"Yes. No. God! I don't know, you're making me crazy." He began pacing the cabin.

"See." She pointed to him. "You don't know how to do this any better than me."

"I know I want you with me."

"So Ayden gets to have everything he wants. Me at the office. Me in your bed. What about what I want?"

"C'mon, Maya. That's not fair. I rewarded you handsomely to get you back at Stewart Investments, and as for being in my bed, you wanted me as much as I wanted you."

Maya turned away from him. He was right. It was unfair of her to put her expectations on him. "You're right. There. Are you happy?"

He stared at her intently. "Not in the slightest. Not unless you're agreeing to come back with me."

"For tonight, yes," she countered. "All my stuff is there."

"And after?" he pressed.

"We'll just have to see."

Have to see? Ayden was still reeling from Maya's words earlier on the plane as he got ready for bed. She'd refused to give an outright yes or no to his request for her to stay with him. Or had he meant *live* with him? He hadn't really defined what he meant. Was that why she was unsure?

Since they'd returned from the airport, he'd been busy catching up on phone calls and emails in his study. There were several from Fallon, as expected. Maybe Maya was right. He should call her, if for no other reason than to make sure she was okay, because despite what he'd said, he did care.

As for Maya, when they arrived, she'd immediately gone upstairs to unpack. Or pack? Ayden didn't have a clue. Just like he didn't know where to go from here. It was all so confusing. Maya was confusing. Bringing her back to Stewart Investments was supposed to be straightforward. He needed an assistant and with a little coaxing she had become available. He'd never anticipated that the attraction he'd felt for her so long ago would rear its ugly head. He'd thought he'd worked through those feelings. It had been a one-time thing because she'd been hurt and he'd wanted to console her. He'd moved on with his life, dated other women and relegated that night to an indiscretion not to be repeated.

He'd never anticipated becoming so taken with her that he'd whisk her off to paradise and make love to her day and night. Or that he would feel a deep yearning to commit to her in some form or fashion.

No one could have foreseen it.

Or could he have? If he'd just dealt with the insatiable lust he'd had for her back then, maybe it would have fizzled out and they'd have gone their separate ways. Now it was complicated because he knew what it was he'd been missing out on all these years. Now Stewart Investments needed her—or rather, *he* needed her—and he'd do anything to keep her.

With renewed purpose, he strode to his library door and took the stairs two at a time until he reached the second floor, where Maya's room was located. The door was ajar and he watched from the doorway as she *unpacked* her suitcase. Surely, this must mean she'd decided to stay? His heart began thundering in his chest, but Ayden refused to analyze what it might mean. "Knock. Knock."

Maya whirled around on her heel to face him. She was holding a sexy little teddy that she'd worn for him in Jamaica, though it hadn't stayed on her long. "Come in."

Ayden smiled as he came toward her, only stopping when he was in her personal space. Maya stepped backward, dropping the teddy, and he advanced. He loved this dance between them. It was a sort of foreplay he would never get tired of. "You're unpacking."

"No, I was just getting out something to wear for tonight…"

He grinned. "Oh really? Well, what do you say you leave that teddy here and come to my room? Because you won't really need it for what I have planned." He circled his arm around her waist and led her out of the room.

"What about dinner?"

"I'll have dinner sent up."

Maya felt oddly out of sorts Monday morning as she went through her usual routine of getting Ayden's calendar settled for the week. Could it be because her sinfully sexy boss and the best lover she'd ever had in her life had kept her up half the night doing wicked things to her? Although she hadn't agreed to move in with him, she had enjoyed the last few nights at Ayden's with unadulterated relish. She even had the whisker burns on her thighs to prove it. Maya blushed. She knew she was expected to jump back into work even after a week and multiple nights spent in Ayden's arms.

He didn't seem to have any problem getting back into the swing of things. She glanced at his door, which had been closed for most of the morning. Ayden had one meeting after another with department heads after their vacation. Eventually the door opened and he emerged. He was wearing a charcoal suit that made him look every bit as powerful as he was. Several other men departed after him.

"Maya, can you come into my office?" He went back inside.

She picked up her tablet and followed him. Ayden

was standing by the floor-to-ceiling windows staring out over Austin.

"Close the door."

She did as instructed and when he spun around to face her there was only one thing she saw in his stare. Red-hot desire. She swallowed.

"Come here." He breathed his command.

Maya battled with herself—her pride demanding that she deny him. He'd already gotten his way by having her stay at his house. She couldn't give him everything. But her own lust for him won out.

She stepped toward him until she was close enough for him to grasp her waist and pull her against him. She arched her neck and glanced up into those eyes she always got lost in. He lifted his hand and curved it around her neck, bringing her face closer to his. Then he bent his head to kiss her until she softened against him. She felt powerless and gave in to the passion he aroused. His lips were firm and sure and took everything. When they broke the kiss, their breathing was shallow and unsteady.

"I've been dying to do that all morning," Ayden said. "I've been in those damn meetings thinking of nothing but kissing you." He stroked her already swollen lips with his thumb.

"We can't do this here." Maya tried pulling away, but Ayden wouldn't let her go.

"You're right. I'm sorry. I should have been more discreet."

She let out a sigh of relief. "Thank you. I don't want everyone to know we're an item." She glanced behind her at the door. "They'll think I got this job back because we're sleeping together."

"But you and I know that not's true. You're back as my EA because you're the best."

"Even better than Caroline?" she asked with a smirk.

His dark eyes stared back at her. "You know the answer to that."

"Good, because this assistant needs to leave early today. My mother is trying a new treatment and I'd like to be there." When they'd been in Jamaica, she'd shared her mother's condition with Ayden.

"Of course. You didn't even need to ask. I wish I had been there when my mom was ill. Take whatever time you need. I'll see you back at the house later?"

She nodded. "Thank you."

He kissed her on the forehead and released her.

After finishing up some last-minute items for Ayden, Maya drove to the cancer center where her mother would be getting her treatments. When she arrived, she found Sophia, Raven and Thomas sitting in the waiting room. They all rose when she approached.

"Maya, I'm so glad you could come," Raven said. "Mama, aren't you happy Maya's here?" Her sister looked up at her and smiled for the first time in a long time.

"You told her about my condition?" Her mother turned to Raven. "I thought you had it covered?"

"Of course, I told her. She had a right to know," Raven responded. "It can't all be me mom, you have another daughter."

"I didn't want Maya burdened especially starting her new job. Or should I say her *old* job." Her mother attempted a laugh, which turned into a coughing fit that required Thomas to help her into a nearby chair.

Maya immediately rushed to her side, kneeling in front of her. "Are you okay?"

"Why are you all hovering over me?" Sophia huffed, coughing again into a handkerchief she pulled out of her purse.

"Because we care," Raven said from beside her. "We all do." She glanced in Maya's direction. "And it's about time you know how much."

Her mother frowned. "What do you mean?"

"It means Maya has been helping pay for your treatments since she returned to Austin. They were too expensive for us to manage with a new baby, and we needed her assistance."

Tears sprang to Maya's eyes. She couldn't believe Raven was taking up for her when she never had in the past.

"So *you're* paying for my continued therapy?" her mother asked, staring at Maya.

"Yes, Mom. I am." Maya wiped away a tear with the back of her hand. "Is that a problem? Or would you rather your favorite daughter and son-in-law continue to struggle?"

"Of course not," Sophia stammered, with tears in her eyes. "I just never thought you cared."

Maya rolled her eyes upward and prayed for strength. She couldn't stand on the sidelines while cancer ravaged her mother. And the monetary assistance wouldn't help only her mother—it was about healing herself. She truly needed to let go of the past. "You're my mother. And although we don't see eye to eye and never have, I do care. I love you."

Tears filled her mother's eyes. "Thank you. I know I may not deserve it, but I'm glad you're here." She squeezed Maya's hand back.

"Good, because you have both your daughters here to support you." Maya glanced over at Raven, who gave her a reassuring smile. They were a long way from reconciliation, but they'd get there. And for the first time in years, Maya was open to it.

A nurse appeared several moments later to take her mother away for the treatment. When they advised that one person could come with her, Maya fully expected Sophia to ask for Raven, but she looked at Maya.

"Would you come with me?"

Maya rose to her feet. "Yes, Mama. I will."

Fourteen

Ayden prowled around his enormous house, glancing at his Rolex every few minutes. It was after eight o'clock and he hadn't heard from Maya. He knew she'd gone to be by her mother's side, but that had been hours ago. She hadn't called or texted and it was driving him crazy. She didn't answer to him after hours, but the least she could have done was let him know everything was all right.

Eventually, after working through the evening, he flopped on the couch and made himself comfortable by turning on the television and flipping through the channels. He never watched TV; it was just noise. Even though he knew his staff was down the hall, he felt lonely without Maya. His voracious hunger for her was not subsiding; he wanted her more than ever. He loved the way she stood her ground, telling him off when she didn't agree with him. Or the way she found joy in the simple things in life like playing dominos or drinking a Red Stripe.

He'd tried to ignore his feelings for Maya, but they kept resurfacing. She was smart and funny and beautiful, with her sexy, tight body. He recalled how she'd looked in a bikini with her skin sun-kissed from the Jamaica sun. He was craving her something fierce and he knew she felt the same, but she was erecting barriers between them. She hadn't agreed to permanently move in with him and had kept her short-term rental. Why was she holding on to it? Was her coming to San Antonio only temporary? It brought a pang to his chest to think of her leaving him. It reminded him of the loss he'd felt when his mother had moved him away from his father, from the only place Ayden had known as home, into a sad one-bedroom apartment. He didn't want to lose Maya. She made him feel alive. Ayden felt like he could do anything when he was with her, like he was worthy. But, more importantly, he'd never been this content or this relaxed with another woman.

He drew a deep, ragged breath. Ayden couldn't remember the last time he'd been truly happy like he'd been these last couple of weeks with Maya. Before her, he'd worked around the clock, stopping only to eat, work out or have the occasional dinner with any number of nameless, faceless women, then leave their beds in the middle of the night. None of them had held a candle to Maya. He stayed with Maya *every night*. He looked forward to drawing her close and spooning with her. And when he did, it was the best sleep of his life.

Eventually, he retired to the master bedroom to shower and get ready for bed. He'd changed into black silk pajama bottoms when he heard Maya's car pull into the driveway. He waited for the click of her heels on the marble floor as she climbed the stairs. Her steps were silent on the plush carpet in the hallway, but he finally sensed her outside his room. Was she trying to decide if she should come in? He hopped off the bed and padded barefoot to her room. "Maya?"

She jumped. "You—you startled me."

"I'm sorry." His gaze swept over her face as he looked for signs of distress. Her eyes were glassy. "Is everything okay? "

She looked downward and when she lifted her head back up, he could see tears staining her cheeks. It made him feel as useless as a rag doll to see her so upset. "Maya, Maya." He pulled her to him, grasping the sides of her face to make her look at him. "Did something happen today?"

She shook her head. "No, it's just…" Hiccupping, she tried to speak through her crying. "I can't…" Her voice trailed off, and she leaned into him and began softly sobbing.

"It's okay." He held her firmly, desperate to give some of his strength to her. "I'm here for you."

When she finally quieted, she spoke softly. "The

treatment they're giving Mom is aggressive. Very aggressive. But it's the only way they can try to rid her of the cancer. It didn't seem real when I found out, but today... There was no denying that my mother could die."

"But she's not going to," Ayden murmured in her ear. "Because of you, she's getting the best treatment available."

"I know that, but it's still so scary. I—I could lose her. And even though we haven't been close, I've always known she was there. And if something happens to her, I'll be all alone because I don't think Raven and I can ever go back to being sisters again, not after her betrayal."

Without hesitation, Ayden said, "You won't be alone, Maya. You'll always have me."

As soon as he said the words, he wished he could take them back.

He wanted them to be true because he cared deeply for Maya, but he couldn't guarantee her that their relationship would always be like this.

He didn't do commitments because there was too great a risk of getting hurt.

Had he just doomed their relationship by telling his first white lie?

You'll always have me.

Ayden's words kept replaying in Maya's head the next day even though she tried to keep her mind on work. Ayden had left hours ago, leaving her to her own devices and thus giving her plenty of time to recount last night. After making love, she'd slept in his embrace as he held her, unable to sleep because his words were in her head like a nursery rhyme she could never forget. She knew he didn't mean them. Couldn't possibly. She didn't have a future with Ayden. She'd been living in an alternate yet blissful universe while ignoring the obvious.

Ayden was an attractive, wealthy man whose interests lay in making money. But it was inevitable that Ayden would return to his former ways. She had to look on their time as the precious gift that it was. He'd made her feel beautiful, sensual and desirable, and she would always be grateful. She would remember their time in Jamaica fondly. The time they'd shared, however, had an expiration date.

Maya was steeling herself for that moment when Ayden would want her to go back to being only his trusted assistant instead of his lover. When he looked to her to make appointments and spreadsheets rather than being desperate for their next kiss or lovemaking session. When she'd have to go back to her boring life in which no other man would ever measure up to Ayden. She knew that when that time came, she'd leave again. There was no way she could see him day in and day out after the time they'd shared. Except this time, she wouldn't go far. Her mother needed her.

She'd started over once. She could do it again. She just didn't want to. She'd set aside most of her sign-on bonus to help with her mother's treatments. There was some left over in her savings, and with her new salary and generous stock options, she could make it until she found a new position.

"I'm back." Ayden startled her as he strode toward her desk.

"How was your meeting?"

"Successful. I convinced Kincaid to bring his portfolio over to Stewart Investments." He grinned from ear to ear. "It was a big day for me."

"That's wonderful, Ayden." She was happy he'd finally landed the elusive client.

"I want to celebrate. What do you say we take off early for a night out on the town?"

Her eyes fixed on his beautiful face and her heart began galloping in her chest. "Why, Ayden, are you asking me out on a date?"

He smiled wolfishly. "Well, ma'am, it appears I am." He rubbed the perpetual five-o'clock shadow on his chin. "Would you like to accompany me to dinner?"

Ayden's infectious mood was catching and Maya felt herself getting excited. "I would love to."

An hour later, Maya was staring back at her reflection in a dressing-room mirror. Rather than navigate the Austin traffic during the middle of rush hour, Ayden had driven her to a stylish boutique where he'd given her her own *Pretty Woman* experience complete with a designer dress purchased right off the rack. Maya had balked at such an outrageous gesture. She had plenty of dresses back at the house, but Ayden wasn't taking her back home. The saleswoman had been happy to assist when he'd pulled out his platinum credit card and told her price was no object.

Now Maya was in a teal halter dress that clung to her slender curves and did wonders for her complexion. She'd touched up her makeup with subtle eye shadow, mascara and lipstick she carried with her. The clerk had insisted she add shoes and a bag, so Maya was ready for the night with a clutch and beaded sandals with straps that wrapped her delicate ankles.

Ayden was waiting for her at the curb, having stepped out to take a phone call earlier while she got dressed. "You look stunning." He whistled as she approached the Bentley.

"You should know. You paid an outrageous sum for this dress."

"I wanted you to not only look good, but feel good."

His words put a smile on her face. "I feel like a million bucks."

"Good." He opened the passenger door and pulled her inside. "Get in."

Ayden took Maya to a popular restaurant known for its wealthy clientele. It was the first time they were going out in public as a couple. Since they'd become lovers, they hadn't been seen by anyone other than the housekeeping staff at the villa in Jamaica and his estate.

Did this mean Ayden might want more from her than a short-lived affair?

Maya didn't want to be hopeful, but it was hard not to read between the lines when he was going out of his way to impress her. First with the couture dress and designer shoes, and now with a fine dining experience. Upon arrival, he showered her with the most expensive bottle of champagne and treated her to the finest meal she'd had in a long time. Each plate was a tiny work of art created by a master chef. Maya felt like she was floating, weightless, carried away on a tidal wave. She knew what was happening. She was falling deeper and deeper in love with Ayden.

Her mind warned her to be cautious, prudent even, to not outwardly portray her true feelings, so she focused on the easy, undemanding conversation they had a tendency to share. She loved the melodic sound and timbre of his deliciously masculine voice. Every now and then she would glance up, only to find his eyes fixed on her, and she was helpless to tear away her gaze.

When the exquisite meal was finally over and they were drinking cappuccino with their intricately conceived desserts, someone called his name. "Ayden!"

Ayden turned and smiled, then rose to his feet to greet half a dozen suited gentlemen coming toward them. It was late, but clearly they'd just had a business meeting. He shook the men's hands. "Good to see you. You enjoyed your dinners?"

"Of course. This place has the best duck in Austin," one of the men answered.

Several of them glanced in Maya's direction and Ayden motioned her over. "Gentlemen, I'd like you to meet Maya Richardson, the best executive assistant in all of Austin."

"Is that why you're taking her out to a meal here?" There were snickers.

Ayden cleared his throat. Maya could see he was

uneasy with the conversation, yet he was allowing it, feeding into it. "You misunderstand. We're colleagues."

Maya was stunned and stared at Ayden in anger and bewilderment. Tears pricked the back of her eyes, but she refused to let these Neanderthals see it. He hadn't even defended her when they had snickered. And she couldn't believe Ayden had just told these men that she meant nothing to him. He might as well as have put a neon sign on her that read Booty Call. Maya had to get away before she said something that embarrassed them both. "Excuse me. I need to visit the ladies' room."

She heard several of the men laugh behind her. "Does she know, Ayden, that you're not the settling-down kind?"

Laughter followed her as she left the dining room, Ayden's included.

Maya nearly slammed the door against the wall as she pushed the door to the restroom open. Not only had Ayden not introduced her as his girlfriend, but he'd laughed about it. Hell, she would have even accepted his describing her as his date, but his *assistant*? Clearly he valued these men's opinions so much that he wasn't even willing to acknowledge she meant more to him than someone who just worked for him. She was furious!

She clasped both her hands to her face and inhaled, trying not to cry. She couldn't make a scene or fall apart. Not here. Not now. Damn! Why did she still care about his reputation after he'd just treated her so shabbily? Because she loved him, and despite everything, she wouldn't embarrass him like he'd just done her. She glanced at herself in the mirror. Her makeup was still intact; she'd held it together. *Just barely.* Now all she had to do was get out there. She just hoped the other men were gone.

As she entered the dining room, she saw Ayden sitting alone. Thank God.

He stood when she approached. "Maya..."

"I'm ready to go." She didn't bother sitting down. "I'd like to go now."

Ayden nodded. "I figured as much and have already taken care of the bill."

Maya didn't wait for him to continue and strode toward the door. She wanted to get away from him as soon as possible. Go back home and lick her wounds. But she wasn't truly going back home. She was going to Ayden's, where she wouldn't have a moment alone to process what had happened.

He must have followed her because he slid beside her at the valet counter, handing the attendant his ticket. Maya folded her arms across her chest and waited for them to fetch Ayden's car. Surprisingly, he was silent beside her. Maybe he knew she was peeved and was in no mood to talk. She did have one question for him.

Why?

Why bring her to a fancy restaurant?

Why romance her at all if all she was to him was a damn good assistant that he just happened to sleep with?

The Bentley arrived at the curb and she didn't wait

for Ayden's assistance. She opened her door herself and slammed it shut. He took the hint and walked around to the driver's side. Once it was just the two of them, he turned to her. "Maya. About earlier… I'm sorry."

"I don't want to talk about it."

"Please don't let what happened ruin a great night."

"You did a fine job of that all by yourself."

She heard him suck in his breath. Score one for her. But she really wasn't interested in winning a battle of wills with Ayden. The real reason she was upset was because he didn't love her. Never would. And she was fooling herself to think otherwise. It was the same as she'd done with Thomas all those years ago. She'd foolishly thought he loved her. When, actually, he'd been sleeping with her sister behind her back. It was humiliating and she'd felt those exact same feelings tonight standing by Ayden's side when he relegated her to nothing more than the help. She couldn't look at him, much less talk to him.

The ride back to his mansion was fraught with tension. As soon as the car stopped, Maya hopped out, but Ayden was hot on her heels. He caught her in the foyer and snagged her hips to him, but she refused to be *handled*. She knew exactly what Ayden would do: he would try to brush aside what had occurred at the restaurant. Make it appear as if she was blowing it out of proportion. And because she was so weak, when it came to him, she'd succumb and he would carry her off to bed where they'd have sex all night long. But then where would they be? Exactly where they'd started.

She continued twisting and turning in his arms in an attempt to get away, but all she did was spin herself around until her backside was against his swelling erection.

"Stop fighting me," he whispered, clasping his arms around her.

"Let me go." Her steely tone must have soaked through his brain, because he released her and they faced off. His hazel eyes were searching her face. For what? She wasn't sure. She just wanted to go to bed. *Alone.*

"I'm going to bed." She grasped the railing of the staircase and started to ascend.

"Maya, I don't want to end the night like this. Can't we talk? Please?" he implored.

She stopped on the staircase. "Talk? About what? That after nearly two weeks spent in bed together that there's nothing between us? Is that what we're going to talk about?"

He frowned. "That's not fair, Maya. Some of them are my colleagues as well as clients. Did you honestly expect me to tell those men that we're an item? To spill my guts to them and tell them how I truly feel?"

She descended the stairs until she was back facing him. "Actually, I did, Ayden. I expected you to acknowledge that I *meant* something to you."

"You do. You know that. I wouldn't have been with you this entire time, giving up work and obligations, if you didn't."

She felt confused. "But yet you couldn't bring your-self to tell those men that you were *with* me, *dating* me. But I get it, okay? What we do in the dark is sup-posed to be for our eyes only and no one else. What I don't understand is why take me out for dinner? Why not just keep me in the house to service you at your beck and call?"

His eyes blazed fury and she could feel the anger emanating from his every pore. "That was a cheap shot, Maya."

"But well deserved." She spun on her heel and ran up the stairs, but Ayden refused to let sleeping dogs lie and she heard his footsteps behind her. When she made it to her room, she slammed the door, shutting him out. She heard the latch give way on the door and sensed Ayden's presence behind her as much as she heard the door click closed behind him. She didn't want to look at him. He'd hurt her. She just wanted to go to bed and forget. To block out the pain until morning, when she would be forced to face re-ality, which was that Ayden was never going to love her.

When Maya began unzipping her dress and it stuck, she let him come behind her and help. He stilled her by placing his hands on her shoulders. Then he easily slid the zip down until he reached her bikini panties. Despite the tension between them, she stepped out of the dress, removed her undies and turned around to face him, naked.

Desire and hunger shot through her as it always did when she looked at him.

Maya didn't speak and neither did he. Instead, she allowed him to tug her toward him until she was lost once again in the bliss she always found in his arms.

Fifteen

The next morning Ayden was gone from her bed before Maya woke up. She was thankful because last night shouldn't have happened. She'd been so upset with him for how he'd treated her in front of his colleagues. How could she have allowed him to make love to her afterward? He must think her a fool, ruled by her libido rather than her head. She'd allowed the physical pull Ayden had on her to make her go completely left when she meant to go right.

After showering and dressing for the day, Maya packed her things. It was time for her not only to get out of Ayden's house, but out of his orbit. She should never have allowed him to convince her to come back to work for him, not with the feelings she'd had. Knowing that he'd desired her, too, did little to soften the blow that Ayden wasn't the type of man she was looking for. And there was no way she could lie or pretend otherwise. If she did, she wouldn't be true to herself and it would suck away her soul.

Maya felt like a raw and open wound. The time they'd shared in Jamaica had been real, so real that it had changed *everything.* Ayden had made her want more than he was capable of giving to her, plain and simple.

Her task was complete in under a half hour because she hadn't brought that many belongings to Ayden's. She called downstairs and the butler ensured her luggage was taken to her car. When she inquired where Ayden was, he informed her he was in the morning room having breakfast. Maya saw no better time than the present to let him know her plans.

She had to do this for her own self-respect and self-worth. Somehow, she'd survive this, just as she had when he'd crushed her spirit five years ago.

She found Ayden reading the newspaper, a cup of coffee along with a half-eaten plate of food on the table in front of him.

He glanced up when she walked into the room. "Good morning." He put down the paper. "I didn't want to wake you, so I came downstairs. I hope you don't mind." He eyed her warily as she sat down next to him.

She shook her head.

"Would you like some breakfast? I can have Cook whip you up something, an omelet perhaps or some crepes. He makes the best crepes you've ever had in your life."

Again, she declined with a headshake. Was Ayden Stewart nervous? Because he was babbling about breakfast when he had to know there was more to be said between them.

"We need to talk."

He chuckled quietly. "Whenever a woman says those words, it can't be good."

She stared at him incredulously.

He held up his hands in defense. "Don't bite my head off. It was just a joke to lighten the mood because I suspect I'm not going to like this conversation very much, am I?"

He fixed his gaze on hers and Maya reminded herself that she'd made up her mind and there was nothing he could do to change it. "I'm leaving and moving back into my apartment."

He nodded. "I suspected as much when I saw your bags were brought down."

"You know why?"

"You're upset about last night. You feel like I disrespected you and this is your way of punishing me."

Maya rolled her eyes in frustration. She wanted to strangle him because he wasn't getting the point. "I'm not trying to punish you, Ayden."

"Then why?" He pounded the table with his fist, startling her. "Why isn't what we have good enough? Why are you leaving me? I know you like it here. *With me.* I know you want to be here and I don't want you to go. So why leave, if not to punish me?"

"Because I want *more*, Ayden. And I'm not willing to take whatever scraps of yourself you're willing to give me."

"I don't understand. What is it that you want? Whatever it is, I'll give it to you."

"Don't you see? You can't. You and I are on different pages. Yes, I've been happy here with you. Cut off from the world in our idyllic little slice of heaven. But it was never real. It was never going to last. I know that and so do you. I want marriage, babies and a white picket fence. I want a family."

"A family?"

"Yes, I've always wanted one. When I was with Thomas, I thought we were headed in that direction. But he went and married my sister and gave her all the things I've always craved. Especially someone to love me." There, she'd said the word aloud. The *L* word that she hadn't dared to speak or make mention of, but she had to now. She couldn't go on making the same bad decisions. Something had to give.

"I wish I could give you all those things, but I can't."

"You mean you *won't*. Because you're not capable of anything more than immediate gratification. And like an idiot, I went along with it, accepting less than what I wanted because I wanted to be with you. Because I never truly got over you the first time." She shook her head. "Why did I do this to myself? Maybe it's because I've never felt like anything special. I never have been for any other man, so why should now be any different? My own mother said as much for most of my life. And as for you, I'm a convenience who just happens to be compatible with you sexually."

"Don't say that!" Ayden shot to his feet. "I don't ever want to hear you say that you're nothing special, Maya. Because you are. You are to me."

Then why won't you love me? She wanted to scream at him, but instead she stared back at him and felt the tears of unrequited love trickle down her face.

"Maya, please don't cry…"

He reached out to touch her, but she bunched her shoulders and moved away. She couldn't let him touch her. Not now. Not when she was weak and vulnerable. He would use it to his advantage to pull her back into his web. She barely had enough strength to have this conversation and demand the things she wanted, whether he was able to give them to her or not.

"It's okay. I walked into this affair with my eyes wide open. I knew who I was dealing with."

He frowned in consternation. "What the hell is that supposed to mean?"

"Nothing." She rose to her feet and began to walk toward the doorway. "I've said what I have to say and it's best I left."

"Oh, no, you don't. You're not getting the last word. At least not until you tell me what you meant."

"You want to go there, Ayden?"

"Yes," he stated unequivocally. His eyes blazed a fire through her.

"All right then. How about we start with the fact that you've never had a serious relationship a day in your life. You flit around from one affair to the next."

"That's because I haven't had the time. I've been building Stewart Investments."

"Rubbish. It's because you're scared. Scared of getting close to anyone or anything because you're afraid of getting hurt. But guess what, Ayden? I'm equally scared, but I'm willing to put myself out there on the off chance that one day—one day—I might find someone who loves me just as much as I love them. And I know that's not you."

"Maya…" His tone softened, "I—I'm just not capable of anything more. I wish to God I were because you're an incredible woman, deserving of happiness. But I just don't believe in happily ever after."

"That's because you're still holding on to the past and the anger you have toward your father. Until you make peace with your family, you'll never be able to move forward."

"You know nothing of my family, not really, other than the few tidbits I told you."

"You're right. I only know the scraps you've chosen to share with me or that I've garnered from working with you all these years, because you've closed yourself off, Ayden. To the world. To your sister, Fallon. And most of all to me. I can't just be the woman you sleep with anymore, no matter how pleasurable that might be. I want more. And I *deserve* it."

"Yes, you do," Ayden said finally in a quiet, defeated tone. "You deserve more than I could ever give you and that, my precious Maya, will be my greatest regret."

Maya nodded and then quietly left the room.

* * *

Ayden stared at the doorway Maya had departed through. He'd been sitting there for the last hour in utter shock. She'd walked out on him. He'd woken up this morning with a deep sense of foreboding of her departure, but he'd told himself it couldn't possibly be true. Maya, *his Maya*, would never leave him. During breakfast, he'd told himself that Maya was upset. Understandably so. He could have handled last night better, but at the time, he just hadn't known what to say.

Were they on a date?

Was she his girlfriend?

They certainly hadn't discussed the ramifications of becoming intimate. Seeing his colleagues had caught him off guard. He'd been that way from the moment she'd walked out of the boutique. She'd looked sensational. Beautiful. Stunning. But mere words did little to describe her. Unfortunately, he'd behaved like an utter jerk. He'd hoped making love would be a salve to her tender spirit, but it hadn't been, even though for him it had been magical. He couldn't recall another time in which he'd felt so connected to another human being.

This morning he'd planned on asking her to make their living arrangement permanent. It was the best he could offer when he didn't do commitments, but for Maya he'd been willing to make an effort. But he hadn't gotten the chance to even ask, because she wanted marriage and babies. And a darn white picket fence! Why did women always want the moon and the stars? Why couldn't she let him have his say and just move in? It might not be exactly what she was looking for, but at least it would have given her some kind of commitment.

But marriage?

Babies?

Oh, hell, no!

Ayden didn't ever plan on getting hitched. He'd seen how married people, supposedly in love, treated each other. When the dust settled, the only ones hurt were the babies, the innocents that had been pulled into their parents' unholy matrimony.

No, thank you. He was content with the single life.

Or at least he had been until Maya had come roaring back into his world with a vengeance.

Now what was he supposed to do? Was she cutting him off entirely? Although, it would be devastating not to make love to her again, he supposed he could get through it if he buried himself in work. But what of Stewart Investments? The last time she'd left him, it hadn't been just him, but her position. It had taken him nearly half a year to find someone. He couldn't go through that again. He *wouldn't* go through that again.

He'd lived with his father's betrayal all these years, accepted he would never be acknowledged as his son. But he couldn't bear it if Maya turned her back on him, too. Because this time, it would destroy him, and Ayden wasn't sure he'd ever recover.

Ayden didn't know what to do. They couldn't go back to their working relationship. They couldn't be lovers anymore. And he doubted she wanted his friendship. There was nothing he could offer her that would entice her to stay and that was the greatest travesty of all.

Maya hated the letter she'd just penned to Ayden and sent by courier. Once again, she'd resigned her position as his executive assistant. The only difference was that this time she was offering her services via virtual assistant until he could find someone permanent. She was prepared to draft his presentations, handle his schedule, make appointments and take his calls *remotely*. She'd thought it through and, logically speaking, they didn't need to see each other. She could do her job without ever laying eyes on him.

It was the best she could come up with on short notice. She knew he was working with several important clients, especially Kincaid, and she was invested in his success. So she was willing to listen to his voice over the phone giving her instructions or read an email with his name on it so long as they had no interaction face-to-face.

She was weak when it came to Ayden. If she were in the office, he'd use every weapon in his arsenal to break down her defenses, and Maya knew herself. Knew she would crumble. So she was offering this olive branch. Either way, the signing bonus was hers free and clear according to the offer letter she'd signed.

She wondered how he would react when he received her resignation. Would he blow his top? Or would he be thankful because she was out of his hair and he wouldn't have to worry about dealing with her demanding any more of him?

Maya found out when her cell phone rang nearly an hour later.

"What the hell is this?"

Maya knew exactly who was on the other end of the line and what he was referring to. "Ayden, you must have received my letter."

"Yes, I did. And I don't accept it."

"C'mon, Ayden. You know it's best if we keep our distance. As a virtual assistant, I can still assist you with the important deals on the table, giving you plenty of time to interview and find my replacement."

"I don't want to replace you, Maya."

She sucked in a breath. "Well, those are your options. You can take them or leave them." She held her breath as she waited for his response.

"I will leave them. Thank you very much. If you want away from me so bad, go ahead, but I warn you, you signed a contract."

"An offer letter," she corrected. "Besides, when I signed, you stated our relationship would be professional only. We crossed that line, Ayden, and no court in the land would uphold that document if they heard what went on between us in Jamaica."

"Damn it, Maya. Don't do this."

"I'm truly sorry, but it's the only way. We both want different things out of life. You're content with the status quo. Me in your bed. While I, on the other hand, lose out on finding my happily-ever-after. Well, no more, Ayden. I'm going to chase after what I want until I find it. Don't stand in my way."

He sighed heavily. There was silence for several long moments in which she heard his slow and controlled breathing before he said, "I will miss you."

"I—I'll miss you, too." Then Maya ended the call. She had to. It was torture to both of them if she let it continue. She would forgive Ayden the same way she had Raven and Thomas, because he was her past and she had to look toward the future. A future that included a husband and children someday. The problem was, her heart was breaking in two and only Ayden could put it back together again. But he wasn't willing or able.

Sixteen

Ayden sat at his desk befuddled. He'd lost ten minutes because he'd been daydreaming about Maya. He told himself it would get better.

But it didn't. The ghost of Maya was everywhere. In his bed. At the office.

He still wanted her, in his life, in his bed, but she wanted marriage and babies. Ayden couldn't give her that. Yet he didn't want to live his life without her. So he'd let her walk away when he didn't want her to go. Did it mean he was in love with her? He wasn't sure. He'd never been in love before. But if there was anyone he wanted to love, it was Maya. He thought about her day and night. And with each passing day, he missed her more and more. Nothing eased the ache in his heart. Not even work, which had been his cure-all for loneliness. The sense of loss was so acute it physically hurt to breathe.

It had been nearly two weeks since Maya had left the mansion, calling him out on his failure to commit. They had been the worst weeks of his life since his mother passed away. Back then, he'd felt alone in the world and emotionally battered. He felt the same way now.

And work was going horribly.

He wished he'd taken Maya up on her virtual assistant offer, but he hadn't. The recruiter had sent a candidate who had emailed the wrong proposals to two different clients earlier in the week. And when he'd yelled at her for the mistake, she'd left the office crying, vowing never to return. The second temp hadn't been much better, but at least she'd lasted a few days. Could no one handle the simple requests he made of them? It was late Friday evening and he would have to muddle through on his own.

Ayden reached for the phone on his desk and called Luke. He didn't care what time it was in London. He needed a sounding board.

"Do you know what time it is?" Luke said.

"No, I didn't look," Ayden responded.

"Well, it's past midnight here," Luke said groggily.

"Sorry."

"No, you're not. So what's going on? I haven't heard from you in over a month so I assumed everything was going swimmingly."

"It was."

"And now it's not?"

Ayden sighed heavily. "Far from it."

"What's happened?"

"Maya left me."

"I could have told you that was going to happen," Luke replied. "It's barely been a month and I bet you ran the poor girl ragged. I warned you about easing up."

"That's not the reason she left."

Silence ensued on the other end of the line before Luke said, "Don't tell me you shagged her again?"

Ayden snorted. "We had a consensual and mutually gratifying relationship. But she still left me. Can you believe it?"

"Are you daft or what, mate? The woman came back because she's had the hots for you, probably did from the get-go, and the first thing you lead with is sex? You don't offer her any kind of commitment other than a good shag—even though you know she's the settling-down kind? Instead, you choose the easy way out? And for the life of me, I don't understand why she went along with it. But go figure. Love is blind."

"Love? No one said anything about love."

"Oh, bloody hell, Ayden! The woman is in love with you. She wouldn't have agreed to come back otherwise. Not after the way you treated her after that one-off five years ago."

"I offered her a lot of money, which she needed to take care of her ailing mother."

"And that might have played a role in her accepting the job, but you and I both know that she came back for *you* and only you. Because deep down she wanted to see if there was a chance for a future with you, and you blew it!"

"Luke, you know I don't believe in love and marriage and all that crap."

"That's a real shame, Ayden, because you're going to miss out on the best thing that ever happened to you, mate."

"Luke…"

"The next time you call me in the middle of night, at least be ready to take my advice. 'Cause right now I'm telling you to sod off," Luke growled.

"Thanks a lot."

"You know I love you like an adopted brother, but I'm going back to bed. Call me tomorrow when you gain some common sense."

Ayden hung up the phone and leaned back in his chair. He felt like all the energy had been zapped out of him. If anyone could give it to him straight and he would listen, it was Luke. With the exception of Maya, Luke was the only person Ayden implicitly trusted.

Was he right?

He'd spent the last fifteen years of life not only surviving, but trying to meet some expectation in his mind that if he was smart enough and rich enough, Henry Stewart would give him the time of day. He had to face facts: Henry was never going to love him. He had to stop looking back on what could have been, *should* have been. It was time to look at what was right in front of him.

Maya.

He'd kept up a shield with every other woman he'd

ever been with, keeping them at arm's length, never allowing them the chance to get close—but not with Maya. He couldn't pretend with this woman. She saw straight through him, not just to his triumphs and successes, but to his failures. She knew he liked his coffee black with two sugars, but she also knew his deep, dark secrets, which made it impossible for him to deny that there was something between them. Something strong and powerful had been forming, but because of Ayden's hang-ups, they were dead in the water. Like Luke, Maya had told him that he needed to resolve his past. Make peace before they could have a future.

Maybe they both had a point.

Ayden knew exactly what he had to do to get started.

Ayden arrived unannounced at Stewart Technologies. He wasn't interested in seeing Henry Stewart, but he was determined to see his sister. After her repeated phone calls, texts and emails had gone unanswered she'd stopped contacting him. And he couldn't blame her; he'd acted like a complete ass toward her. He couldn't give her the financial bailout she needed, but at the very least, he owed her an apology for ignoring her.

When he told her assistant that he was her brother, however, the woman politely said, "Nice try." Fallon had one brother and that was international superstar Dane Stewart. But Ayden hadn't budged from the spot until she'd finally agreed to tell his sister he was standing outside her door.

In time, Fallon emerged from her office in an elegant red pantsuit. Her blond-streaked brown hair was flat ironed and her makeup was flawless. She was the epitome of class and sophistication. She stood in the doorway and regarded him. "I'm shocked you've deigned to darken my doorstep, Ayden Stewart."

"I deserve that," Ayden said, walking toward her, "but I'd like to talk if you have a moment."

Fallon glanced at her assistant. "No interruptions, please. My brother and I have some unfinished business."

Ayden couldn't resist a smirk as he passed the woman, whose mouth hung open in shock. He strode into the room, and Fallon closed the door behind him. Then she folded her arms across her chest and stood rooted to the spot.

"I have to admit, big brother, I'm surprised you've come into enemy territory. Because that's what I am to you, right? Your enemy. So what gives? Why are you here? And what's happened to you? You look god-awful!"

Ayden knew he looked tired and there were lines under his eyes. He hadn't slept in the weeks since Maya left him. He answered her first question. "You're not my enemy, Fallon."

She rolled her eyes upward. "You could have fooled me, Ayden. Your actions speak louder than any words. And, trust me, those were enough. I know my mother did yours wrong and you blame my family for every bad thing that happened in your life. But guess what, Ayden? I didn't harm you. I wasn't even born when all that went down. Yet you blame me as if I had some control over the past."

"You're right."

"Excuse me?"

"I said you're right," Ayden replied, raising his voice. "I was wrong to blame you, Fallon. You and Dane are innocent in this." She nodded but didn't speak, so he continued. "Our parents are to blame for what went down back then, and I'm sorry that I put you in the middle of that. You've tried to extend an olive branch to me and I've never wanted to take it."

"Because you're angry that I got the life denied you?"

"Yes." Ayden was man enough to admit that. "You and Dane not only got my father—" Ayden beat his chest with his fist "—but you got the good life. The houses, the cars, the travel, the fancy clothes and schools. While I had to work my butt off for everything I've ever achieved."

"But I bet it's all the more sweet," Fallon replied.

"What do you mean?"

"I know you had a hard life," she responded. "But my life hasn't been a picnic, either. I admit I've had every material possession, but you want to know something? I've also had a disinterested, self-absorbed mother who couldn't be bothered to raise the two children she had in order to keep our demanding father. And Henry Stewart? He hasn't been an easy man to love, constantly pushing me to excel. I've had to bust my tail for years to prove I'm the best person to run this company. I've always been in Dad's shadow, unable to run Stewart Technologies how I see fit without constant input and criticism. And right when I make it to the top, I see my whole life's work on a weak foundation and the sand is crumbling underneath my feet."

Fallon walked over to the couch and sank down onto it.

Ayden rushed over. "I had no idea how hard it's been on you."

"Father wanted Dane to take over the company, but my baby brother is only interested in making movies. He's never wanted to be a businessman, much to father's chagrin."

"So he pushed you."

"Yes. And don't get me wrong, I love what I do. And I love this company. It's why I came to you for help."

"And I turned my back on you," Ayden replied. "I'm sorry for that, Fallon. It's just that..."

She reached for his hands and grasped them. "It's okay. I had no right coming to you. Not after what father did to you. But I felt I had no choice and was out of options. The reason I called was to let you know I'd had it out with my mother and she admitted to ensnaring father. I only wanted to say that I was sorry."

"Thank you for that," Ayden said. Hearing that Nora had admitted to part of the blame was something, but what about Fallon? "What are you going to do about the company? If you really need the money, I could loan it to you. Not to the company directly, but as a personal loan with a good interest rate."

"Ayden, that's very generous of you considering the circumstances, but I could never accept, not knowing how Daddy treated you and your mother. This isn't your cross to bear. It's mine."

"But you're my sister."

"And I will find a way and might already have. Anyway, the fact that you've come here today—" her voice caught in her throat "—you have no idea how much this means to me."

"It means a lot to me, too, Fallon. I've been alone for a long time. Hell, since before my mother even passed. And, well, I've felt adrift without a family, but if you and Dane are willing... I'd like to try to have a relationship with you both." He was never going to forgive Henry for abandoning him or his mother, but he could try to forge a bond with his siblings.

A warm smile spread across her lips. "Ya know, I wouldn't mind having a big brother. Someone I could look up to. Maybe even call for advice?"

Ayden returned her grin. "I'd like that. I'd like that very much."

Fallon glanced down at her watch. "Now I have to get to a meeting, so let's plan on having dinner sometime soon, okay? I won't push. We can do this in baby steps."

"Baby steps." Ayden laughed. He opened his arms and, after several seconds, Fallon came into his embrace, returning his hug. It was a small gesture, but meant everything to Ayden.

After leaving Stewart Technologies, Ayden felt a heavy burden had been lifted off his shoulders. Clearing the air with Fallon and agreeing to start anew as a family was one the best decisions he'd made in a long time. He hadn't realized just how much the hatred and anger was eating him up inside and taking up room in his heart. To acknowledge that he needed Fallon and Dane was a big step for him. He was used to being on his own, staying in control, feeling nothing, but being with Maya had changed him.

He'd been pretending for years that Maya was just an assistant, a friend, even a lover, but she was more than that. She was everything to him. He had to talk to her. Tell her that he was a fool. Tell her that he loved her. Tell her she was his other half, his soul mate, and pray that she would take him back. He was prepared to lay down every vestige of his pride, *do anything*, if she'd just give him another chance.

It was essential that Maya keep her mind occupied. It was time she got settled and moved on with her life. It had taken a couple of weeks, but she'd found a permanent apartment in an area of Austin she liked and given up her short-term rental. Callie had driven from San Antonio to help her unpack her belongings from storage over the weekend so it would feel like home.

Maya had to admit the added benefit of being in Austin was that she was closer to Sophia. She'd already been able to make it to her mother's last couple of treatments.

This time she wasn't running from her problems. She was sticking around to spend time with her mother and develop some semblance of a relationship with Raven. Just that weekend, she'd met up with her sister at a baby store to shop for baby clothes and they'd gone for coffee afterward, which allowed Maya to coo over her niece. It was a small step toward mending their relationship, but one she never would have taken if she hadn't come back home.

She wasn't desperate for money, and was keeping herself busy until she could find a new job. Busy cleaning and decorating her new home. Grocery shopping to fill her refrigerator. Running in the early-morning hours. Focused on the books she read. Any activity she could think of that would take up room in her mind. Because if she didn't, the memories would arrive. And what purpose was there in reliving the nights she'd spent making love with Ayden. Because that's exactly what it had been. It hadn't been sex.

She was in love with Ayden and had given him a part of herself, but he didn't love her back. What was wrong with her? Why couldn't she find a man who would love her? She'd thought Thomas had, but he'd chosen Raven over her. And now Ayden. He was everything she wanted and could ever need. She wanted to be his wife, the mother of his babies, but he didn't want her forever. Just right now. It made Maya realize that she'd never really loved Thomas because he paled in comparison to Ayden, the man she'd secretly loved for the last decade. And she had to face the facts: she couldn't force him to love her back. She had to accept that he was never going to love her like she loved him. Heck, he didn't want to even try. She understood he'd been hurt, but would he ever allow love in?

Thoughts of Ayden were still invading her subconscious on Monday morning when she started a temp job a headhunter found for her. Maya tried to block Ayden from her mind and concentrate on typing. Tap, tap, tap on the keyboard. She could and would do what was necessary to move forward by keeping focused on the spreadsheets and reports she was assigned.

The elevator door chimed and Maya didn't know what made her look up. Maybe it was the powerful force field surrounding Ayden that required her absolute attention. Because there he was, striding toward her desk. Maya's stomach hollowed at the sight of him. She tried to quell the feeling, but there was no point. The effect of seeing him after weeks of going without was too much.

Ayden was standing in front of her in the flesh!

The man she'd loved, who'd once held her in his arms, kissed her passionately, made love to her tenderly, cuddled with her quietly was here. He'd been her entire universe that week in Jamaica. She would have probably continued to carry on their affair, grateful for whatever piece of himself he was willing to give her. Who knew how long she would have gone? "How did you find me?"

"An investigator."

"Why? We're over, Ayden. There's nothing left to be said."

"I disagree. I need to talk to you," he whispered.

She chuckled to herself at his arrogance, but why should she be surprised? "It's always about you, isn't it? Well, no more, Ayden. I choose me and my happiness. You should go."

"That's fair, but I'm not leaving. If I have to, I'll camp out until we have an opportunity to talk. I miss you, Maya."

A tear slipped down her cheek at his honest admission. "All right, we can talk."

She moved from behind the desk and walked toward the elevator. Ayden's hand closed around her elbow.

"I miss you, too, by the way," Maya commented, giving him a sideways glance, "but that changes nothing."

Ayden snorted. "It changes everything, Maya. It means there's still a chance."

"A chance for what?" She sniffed.

"For us."

They were silent as they waited for the car. Maya didn't know what to say. She had no idea why Ayden had come. She still wanted love and commitment, marriage and children. The whole enchilada. And she wasn't willing to settle for less.

The elevator arrived and Maya stepped in. She stole a glance at Ayden and found his eyes fixed on her. Watching her. She didn't want to look too closely at him. She would hear what he had to say and then leave. The car dinged again and several more people entered, forcing Ayden to move closer. Far too close for her liking. Her breath tightened in her lungs at his nearness.

The ride ended several moments later. Maya walked quickly through the lobby toward the revolving doors and across the cascade of steps that led to a large courtyard housing a green space where workers came to eat their lunch. Since it was still late morning, it was deserted.

Maya broke away and sat on a nearby stone bench. She needed to put distance between them. It hadn't been long enough for her to become immune to being near him. As it was, she'd had a hard time in the elevator because she'd felt his hard chest pressed against her back as it became overcrowded.

"What do you want, Ayden? I thought our conversation at your mansion and then again over the phone was pretty clear."

"Not quite," he responded, taking a seat beside her. "There's a lot I need to say to you and you need to hear."

She shrugged. "All right, I'm all ears."

He turned to face her. "For years, I was used to not having any emotions because feelings equaled weakness. If my stepfather saw me have any kind of emotion whatsoever when he was verbally abusing my mother or smacking us around, he'd hit us harder. Yell louder. So I learned to control my emotions to show none. Become impenetrable so I wouldn't get hurt."

"I'm sorry, Ayden. I can't even imagine how horrible it was. But I still don't understand what this has to do with us."

"A lot, if you'll give me a chance to explain. When you walked into my office ten years ago, I sensed you were something special, someone different from the other women I'd met. You weren't looking for anything from me, so you fit perfectly as my assistant.

But as the years went on, you became less of an assistant. You became my friend." When she began to speak, he held up his hand. "I know I made your life hell back then. Having you send flowers and gifts to my dates. I think in my own way I was trying to test you to see if you would crack and throw yourself at me, but you never did. You just quietly let me be myself. Soon, I was opening up to you about the childhood I'd endured. I know it wasn't everything, but it was more than I'd told anyone."

"I remember I was surprised when you shared your story with me."

"You listened. You didn't judge or offer platitudes. It meant the world to me. And I think part of me knew that I had to keep you at arm's length. Otherwise, I would fall head over heels for you."

"But you didn't, Ayden."

"Five years ago, you cracked my armor when you came to me distraught over Thomas. I honestly never meant for anything to happen between us. I wanted to comfort you. Make you see how beautiful you were inside and out. And then you kissed me. Leading to the most spectacular night of my life up to that point."

"Yet you still showed me the door," Maya pressed. She hadn't forgotten the hurt she'd felt.

"Because I was scared. Scared of the feelings you'd evoked in me. Feelings I'd never felt before with another woman. So, of course, I did what I knew best. I pushed them down. Acted as if they didn't exist. I hurt you immeasurably and you left, with good reason. But then you came back, and all those old feelings resurfaced, Maya." He leaned in to cup her face with his large hands. "Don't you see they'd never really left? They'd been buried this entire time. But that week in Jamaica brought them to the forefront. It changed everything. I could no longer hide how much I wanted to be near you, mouth to mouth, skin to skin. I finally had you in my life and didn't want to let you go."

"Neither did I. You made me ridiculously happy in Jamaica and afterward. I thought surely you must feel something. Maybe even love me, just a little. But then you were willing to let me walk out the door, out of your life."

"I'm sorry, Maya. I was afraid I wouldn't be able to give you everything you might need. Marriage? Children? It terrifies me because I never wanted to do what my father did to me, Maya. He ripped me apart. Destroyed our family. Took away my home. Abandoned me. Gave away *my* inheritance to his new family. Never acknowledged me."

She touched his cheek with her hand. "Then don't be that man, Ayden. Be better than him."

He nodded and she saw tears glistening in his eyes. "It's why I'm here. I took your advice. I met with Fallon and we talked. We're going to try to make a go of this brother-sister thing. Hopefully, Dane will be on board, too."

"And your father?"

He shook his head. "That ship sailed a long time ago, Maya. And I can live with that. What I can't live without is you. I love you, Maya. And if you'll have me, I want to be your friend, your lover, your partner, your *husband*."

A sob worked its way upward and she let it out. *Had she really heard him correctly?* "Husband?"

"Yes, I want to spend the rest of my life with you, Maya. I don't want my life to be consumed with work. I want it to be full and rich. I want someone to share it with. I want you. Please tell me it's not too late. Though even if it is, I'm going to try my best to win you over."

She placed her palm flat on his chest. "You don't have to try to win me over, Ayden. You've had me from the moment I stepped foot in your office ten years ago and every moment thereafter. I love you. I always have and I always will."

Her entire body swayed toward his and Ayden swept her into his arms, kissing her fiercely, passionately. His faint stubble teased her skin and she moaned at the realization of a dream come true. When they finally parted, he reached into his suit pocket, and before she knew it he was down on one knee, pulling out a ring box. "Will you marry me, Maya? Will you make me the happiest man on earth by agreeing to grow old with me and have lots of babies that look just like you?"

With the back of her hand, Maya wiped the tears that were sliding uncontrollably down her face. "Yes, yes, yes, I'll marry you, Ayden."

His mouth moved over hers, slow and warm. "I promise I will treasure you for the rest of our lives."

"As will I. You won't be alone anymore, Ayden, because we're family."

"And you, my dear Maya, are my home. I love you."

Epilogue

"I can't believe I'm going to meet *the* Dane Stewart," Maya said when she and Ayden sat down to dinner at an exclusive restaurant in Austin known to cater to the wealthy. "And that we'll be related!"

"That's right." Ayden smiled. He couldn't wait to make Maya his wife. She would be his and vice versa. Since they'd gotten engaged several weeks ago, he'd been eager to get started planning their wedding. He was just sorry he'd wasted so much time, taking five long years before he'd finally admitted that she was the best thing to ever happen to him. But they were together now and that's all that mattered.

"Are you nervous?" Maya asked, peering up at him from under thick lashes.

Maya was intuitive. She must have noticed him

tapping his foot underneath the table. "I would say I'm anxious," Ayden responded evenly. "Fallon has always been open to accepting me as her brother while Dane, up to this point, has steered clear of the family, same as me. So I don't know what to expect."

"You can expect that I won't judge you for our parents' shortcomings," a deep male voice said from behind him, "like you did Fallon."

"Dane!" Fallon muttered from behind him, swatting him on the arm. "You promised to behave." She wore a scowl that didn't match the vibrancy of her orange midi-dress, which was tailored to perfection on her slender figure.

"I was just joking," Dane said, laughing as he turned to face her.

Ayden rose to his feet and faced his baby brother. Dane Stewart was as tall as Ayden, well over six feet, with an athletic physique hidden in all-black attire: jeans, T-shirt and leather jacket. He had the same caramel complexion as Fallon, but didn't share Ayden and Fallon's eye color. His were dark brown and mischievous. Ayden could see why he was America's favorite actor.

"Dane." Ayden offered his hand and Dane snorted.

"We're brothers, Ayden. I think a hug is in order."

Ayden was stunned when Dane walked toward him and wrapped his arms around him in a bear hug. He'd never had a family before. Never thought he'd ever have one. Or even needed one. But now that they were here, Ayden wondered how he'd ever survived like that. He patted Dane's back. "Yes, we are. Yes, we are."

They parted, and a surge of emotion welled in Ayden. He could feel tears at the back of his eyes. Sensing he was overcome, Maya came and stood beside him, sliding her hand into his. It was a simple act, but meant the world to him. He smiled down at her and she rewarded him with a beaming grin.

"Where's the champagne?" Dane glanced around for the waiter. "I believe there's an engagement to celebrate."

"Bring it on," Fallon concurred with a grin. "It's time we welcome Maya into the family."

As champagne soon followed, Ayden sat back in his chair and thought about how thankful he was to finally get to know the brother and sister he'd once refused to claim, with the woman he loved by his side. Life couldn't get any better.

* * * * *

Don't miss Fallon's story,
coming soon
from Yahrah St. John
and Harlequin Desire.

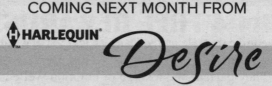

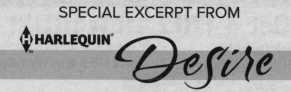
They'd never talked about how they were always overlapping
each other with dating other people.

It was an odd thing to notice.

Why had Sabrina noticed?

Sabrina Douglas was his best girl friend. Girl, space,
friend. But Flynn felt a definite stir in his gut.

For the first time in his life, sex wasn't off the table for
him and Sabrina.

Which meant he needed his head examined.

After the tasting, Sabrina chattered about her favorite
cheeses and how she couldn't believe they didn't serve wine
at the tour.

"What kind of establishment doesn't offer you wine with
cheese?" she exclaimed as they strolled down the boardwalk.
Which gave him a great view of her ass—another part of her
he'd noticed before, but not like he was noticing now.

Not helping matters was the fact that he didn't have to wonder what kind of underwear she wore beneath that tight denim. He knew.

They'd been friends and comfortable around each other for long enough that no amount of trying to forget would erase the image of her wearing a black thong that perfectly split those cheeks into two biteable orbs.

"What do you think?" She spun and faced him, the wind kicking her hair forward, a few strands sticking to her lip gloss. He reached her in two steps. Before he thought it through, he swept those strands away, ran his fingers down her cheek and tipped her chin, his head a riot of bad ideas.

With a deep swallow, he called up ironclad Parker willpower and stopped touching his best friend. "I think you're right."

His voice was as rough as gravel.

"You're distracted. Are you thinking about work?"

"Yes," he lied through his teeth.

"You're going to have to let it go at some point. Give in to the urge." She drew out the word *urge*, perfectly pursing her lips and leaning forward with a playful twinkle in her eyes that would tempt any mortal man to sin.

And since Flynn was nothing less than mortal, he palmed the back of her head and pressed his mouth to hers.

Don't miss what happens next!
Best Friends, Secret Lovers *by Jessica Lemmon,*
part of her Bachelor Pact series!

Available February 2019 wherever
Harlequin® Desire books and ebooks are sold.

www.Harlequin.com

Love Harlequin romance?

DISCOVER.

Be the first to find out about promotions,
news and exclusive content!

 Facebook.com/HarlequinBooks

 Twitter.com/HarlequinBooks

Instagram.com/HarlequinBooks

Pinterest.com/HarlequinBooks

ReaderService.com

EXPLORE.

Sign up for the Harlequin e-newsletter and
download a free book from any series at
TryHarlequin.com.

CONNECT.

Join our Harlequin community to share
your thoughts and connect with other
romance readers!
Facebook.com/groups/HarlequinConnection

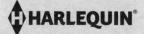

**ROMANCE WHEN
YOU NEED IT**